Salto turned to Gort. 'I gave this guy five hundred quid to get a certain article from ILR. There was to be another five hundred when he delivered. But he didn't show. He got scared out of his tiny mind. He got in on the Scotch till it was coming out of his ears. And then he did a very silly thing. He got the sack . . .

'But the money had to run out some time, didn't it? And then you ran for the big city, the lights, or maybe you had a friend here.' Salto spread his hands. 'My, my. Right on our doorstep. Didn't you know that, dear Heart? Didn't you know we kept open house?'

Gort moved then, over to the sideboard. He took a glass and tapped it steadily against the shelf.

'We had a little ugly this morning, didn't we?' Salto said.

Gort tapped the glass harder. It broke, leaving a jagged edge.

'And what I want you to do,' Salto said, 'is go back to that company called ILR and collect that certain article.'

'I can't go back there,' Hiller told him, 'not now.'

'Not now. Tomorrow.' Salto made it a fact. 'I mean, they know you there. They'll let you in. You'll just have to think of some excuse.'

'It's not that easy. You . . .'

Gort came towards him with the broken glass.

'We don't want to have a *very* ugly,' Salto said. 'Do we?'

By the same author

Bandersnatch
The Boondocks

DESMOND LOWDEN

BELLMAN AND TRUE

A Thames Mandarin Paperback

A Thames Mandarin Paperback

BELLMAN AND TRUE

British Library Cataloguing in Publication Data

Lowden, Desmond
  Bellman and true.
  I. Title
  823'.914[F]   PR6062.088

  ISBN 0-423-02020-X

First published 1975
by Eyre Methuen Ltd
This edition published 1987
by Methuen London Ltd
in association with
Thames Television International Ltd
149 Tottenham Court Road, London W1P 9LL
reissued in 1989 by Thames Mandarin
Michelin House, 81 Fulham Road,
London SW3 6RB

Copyright © 1975 Desmond Lowden

Copyright © Ain't she sweet, 1927
Used by kind permission of CBS Songs

Printed and bound in Great Britain
by Cox & Wyman Ltd, Reading

for Ivor, with thanks for the constable's torch
for Nick, with thanks for the tortoise

Yes, I ken John Peel and Ruby too.
Ranter and Ringwood, Bellman and True.
From a find to a check, from a check to a view,
From a view to a death in the morning.

1

The man and the boy walked down the street with their cases. It was dark, October had come suddenly to London. And it was quiet, the Earl's Court hotels were small and sad. One of them on the corner had a cold blue sign, Hotel Marina, and a card in the doorway saying Vacancies.

The man led the way over. He was middle-aged, with thinning hair, but there was something of the schoolboy about him. It was the tweed suit, ready-made, from a High Street tailor's. The sort of suit you bought on leaving school for your first job. The man had kept to the same style ever since, though heavier now in the stomach and seat. And he'd looked after them well, as he walked he kept the suitcases carefully away from his trouser creases.

The boy followed. He was small, the back of his head was soft and rounded. But his face was pale, sharply pointed with the effort of being ten years old.

They stopped outside the hotel. The man, whose name was Hiller, looked down at the boy a moment. 'What shall we call ourselves this time?' he asked. 'Hawkins? Mr J. Hawkins? Will you remember that?'

The boy nodded. He didn't seem surprised.

Hiller looked up the street and down, carefully, into the shadows. He told himself they couldn't have followed him here. He'd shaken them off yesterday and he'd had twelve clear hours start.

He went up the steps and through window in the hallway slid back. A th moustache looked out.

'D'you have a double room?' Hille beds?'

'A double room?' The man frowned at the boy.

'He's my son,' Hiller said.

'His mother isn't with you?'

'She's not well. We had a holiday booked in the West Country, off-season. She said we'd be stupid not to go. We're on our way back . . .' Hiller tailed off, knowing he'd said too much.

The man nodded and looked down at a chart. It had entries in pencil, and the paper was grey with rubbing out. 'You can have Number 5,' he said. 'That's £8.00 a night, Continental Breakfast included.' He was still looking at the boy. His eyes seemed hurt, always hurt by people who took double rooms at £8.00 a night.

They went up the stairs. The banisters, and each landing they came to, were boxed in with hardboard. The whole house seemed to be divided into little boxes, with green Exit lights flickering in the twilight.

The room, when they reached it, was small. There was an old striped carpet, and a basin in the corner held up by its plumbing. Hiller went straight to the window. He stood close to the glass and smelt the sourness of other people's breath. Across the street he saw the four houses in a row that were empty, their insides gutted and piled at the kerb, their windows dark. And Hiller felt safe. No-one could see he was here.

'That's fine,' he said. He hadn't looked at the room itself, at the stained wallpaper, or the chair that sagged to the shape of a big man.

The manager stared at him strangely. 'Continental Breakfast from eight to nine. That's a couple of bits of toast, and coffee or tea.'

'Fine.'

'I'll say goodnight, then.' The man put the key on the bedside table and went out. Hiller went to the door after him and locked it.

'Not much, is it?' The boy looked round. 'Not what call much, exactly.'

'o.'

'Not after the hotel in Torquay. That was all right.'

'And I'm not having you ringing down for Cokes in the middle of the night,' Hiller said. 'Not any more.'

'There's no bell here.'

'That's good.' Hiller stood under the light, filling his pipe from a pouch. He had slabby white fingers, engineer's fingers, and they moved carefully. He was a pale man, overweight, who in his forty-two years had never looked for sunlight or exercise. And if his face was weak, if it began every day with a hangover, then his neatness – the carefully hung suit and the clean shirt he put on each morning – was the way he rode over it. His mouth was downturned, hurt even, where once it had only been shy. Not long ago people had been able to pierce that shyness after a few drinks and find the humour beyond. It was only in the last two years that the hard sour lines of worry had come. And now the fear.

'I'm going to wash.' He opened his case, felt through the clean shirts until he found the towel. It was wrapped in the shape of a bottle. He took it, and his sponge-bag, out of the door. When he came back he smelt of peppermint.

The boy grinned at him. He too had his case open now. Expensive toys gleamed in the faded room – a speedboat, a model racing car, and a fire engine that steered by a cable. Together they'd cost £98. The boy held the racing car up to the light. There wasn't a scratch on it.

'You do take care of your toys.'

'Yes, I do.' He nodded. 'That is one thing.'

'Are you hungry yet?' Hiller looked down at the small dark head. His voice was softer since his visit to the bathroom.

'I don't know. What we got?'

'You did the shopping.'

'Oh, yeh.' The boy put the car down and reached round for a carrier bag. He got out a Kellogg's Variety Pack, two éclairs, and a rye loaf. The rest were tins – Vulcano Boiled Lentils, Old South Pickled Canteloupe, Fruit Cocktail In Heavy Sauce, Ladies' Fingers in Brine, and Colman's OK

9

Fruity Sauce. They'd been round the delicatessens.

Hiller found the two enamel plates they'd bought. The boy found the tin-opener. 'You want some?' He opened the Ladies' Fingers and sniffed at them.

'Not right now.' Hiller was peering through a gap in the curtains at the street. He turned and picked up the wrapped towel again. 'I'm going to get some water from the bathroom.'

'There's water here.'

'Not drinking water. That's in the bathroom.'

The boy shrugged. 'You don't have to go there. You know that.'

For a moment Hiller's face was concerned. Then he went out of the door. When he came back he was breathing more easily, and the peppermint smell was strong. The boy was surrounded by open tins.

'Supper all right?'

'Not bad.'

Hiller started unpacking his case. He laid his shirts carefully in the wardrobe drawers. And he spent a little time there, hidden by the door, drinking from the wrapped bottle.

When he looked round, the boy was moving away from the picnic towards one of the divan beds. 'All right if I get into bed with my shoes on?' he asked.

'I should think so.'

The boy pulled back the sheet and got into bed fully clothed, moving around to see how it felt. Then, watching Hiller, he got ten Gold Leaf from his pocket. 'All right if I smoke?'

'Go ahead.' Hiller sat by the window. Again he opened a crack in the curtains and looked down at the street.

The boy lay on his stomach, smoking a cigarette he didn't enjoy, turning the pages of a war comic he couldn't read. His head was quite still, clenched against one dirty fist. Hiller waited. He knew what was coming next.

'How much pocket money do I get tomorrow?'

'That depends.'

'Depends on what?'

'If you don't run away.'

The boy turned, his eyes screwed up against a curl of smoke. He held the cigarette away, he wanted to concentrate. '£10.00 for the day? If I don't run away?'

'£5.00.'

'£7.50.'

'All right.' Hiller felt a moment's fear. There weren't many seven pounds fiftys left in his pocket. He didn't want to think about tomorrow. 'You must have got quite a lot of money by now,' he said.

'I'm saving up.'

'What for?'

'You know, the cabin cruiser.'

'That big one, you mean?'

'It is quite big,' The boy nodded. 'Three feet long.'

'And expensive for a toy.'

'£139.90. But it's radio-controlled,' the boy went on quickly. 'Left and right rudder, forward and reverse engines, and a searchlight.'

'There's that, I suppose.'

For a moment there was silence.

'Why d'you keep running away?' Hiller asked then.

'I don't know.'

'Don't you like being on holiday?'

'Oh, that? Yeh, I like that. It's just . . .' The boy looked for somewhere to put his ash.

'On the carpet,' Hiller said.

Then suddenly the dark eyes were looking at him, level with the mattress. 'She isn't well, is she? Mum, I mean? That's all it is?'

Hiller stared at the pale face that narrowed to a pointed nose, flaking at the tip, as though boring a path through a strange hard world. 'She isn't well,' he said.

And they both wanted to believe that.

Later, the light was out and the curtains drawn back. Hiller was in the shadows by the window, the bottle hidden under his chair.

The boy watched him. He knew all about this time of the evening, when the room got thick with smoke and the smell of liquor. He watched the neatness go out of the man, his hands fumbling as he spilled sparks from his pipe, his hair falling away from the careful brushstrokes that hid his baldness. 'Tell me a story,' he said.

'Don't know any stories.'

The voice was slurred. The boy knew the time was right. 'Yes, you do,' he insisted.

'If you say so.'

'Come on.'

'Cowboy story?' Hiller tried. 'The one about Pissoff the Peon? Shot people from behind, mostly in the stomach?'

'Not that one.'

'All right. The one about the vicar, who always wore slippers with bunnies on them?'

'Not that one.'

'What one then?'

'You know.'

Hiller sat back, his pipe sappy between wet lips. 'The Continuing Saga of Sod's Law,' he said at last. 'You Can't Win.'

'That's the one.'

'Where'd we got to?'

'This place with the sign outside,' the boy said. 'It was called Lulu Land.'

'Ah, yes. Lulu Land.' Hiller nodded. 'Short Life beer, fourpence a pint, all cheques accepted. And the juke box played nothing but Wagner, went through Tristan from the overture on.'

The boy didn't understand. 'Who was there?' he asked.

'The usual people. Sooty-Ann Gorge, Mousey Tongue, and Alcide Slow Drag Pavageau.'

'And the Princess?'

'Yes.' Hiller sighed, a short flat sound in the darkness. 'She was there.'

'The Princess who smoked French cigarettes? And was

12

beautiful when she wasn't looking?'

'That's the one.' Hiller's hand shook as he picked up the bottle.

The boy was silent. He'd known the Princess too. 'And was I there?' he asked finally.

'Course you were.' The warmth of the whisky got into Hiller's voice. 'We were all there. We played Skittles and Brittles and One Jump Ginger. And we had a dog that ate nothing but Income Tax Men.'

'What else did we do?'

'Sometimes we'd go out in our Hupmobile. We'd have our pints in quart mugs so they didn't spill while we were driving. And when we got back we'd light the fire with coal-bills. It was good there. We only had one rule. We didn't let in anyone who had a Rover TC.'

'A Rover what?'

'TC. A Rover Tinear Cruoris.'

'What's that?'

'I'll tell you.' Hiller spoke louder suddenly. 'People with Rover Tinear Cruoris's live in four-bedroom fake Georgian houses. They marry St Bernard dogs called Darling, and they have nasty little kids in green jump-suits who come in through the window on a wire, and say Gosh and all that sort of *thing*.' There was real anger in his voice. 'What's more, they keep a cross-index file on everyone earning more than thirty grand in the Southern Counties. And if you mention Stoke Poges, they say you must know Mannering.'

The boy sat forward, not understanding, but drawn to the anger because it was like a child's. 'And then?'

'Well, we made just the one mistake in this place of ours,' Hiller said. 'We let this man in, and we didn't know he had a Rover Tinear Cruoris. He didn't seem like it at first. The Princess liked him. He had things weighed up, you see. He had a camel hair coat, and he knew the going price of Manganese.'

'But the Princess wouldn't have liked any of that.' The boy was hurt. 'She wouldn't have liked him at all.'

'No, she wouldn't.' Hiller's voice was soft as he lied.

Because he'd been just one of the men the Princess had liked. She'd always surprised him, every time.

'Let's kill him off,' the boy said, 'with a digger-tractor, sharp, and with bits of stones sticking to it.'

'That's it,' Hiller said.

The boy was asleep now, and Hiller was trying to hold on to his fear. He had the empty bottle across his knees, and he was staring out of the window.

He told himself he'd chosen right. There were just the dark windows across the street. And the new signs, as yet unlit, of the hotel they were building from the four empty houses. He told himself Gort couldn't have followed him here.

But in a room down the street past the new hotel, Gort was watching. He had the wall-phone in his hand. 'I'm sure it was him went in there,' he said. 'And look, I'll need help. Could you get someone else over? I could easy lose him in the morning.'

2

Hiller woke with a fur lining to his mouth, and a head and a stomach that were two separate parts, far away. He tried to get them together as he turned round to look at the other bed.

It was empty.

Hiller sighed. He got up queasily and went to the basin. He used cold then hot water on his head before shaving. He put on a clean shirt, he put on the suit he'd hung up carefully before going to bed, he brushed his hair over his growing baldness. And he told himself he felt better.

Then he looked at the boy's suitcase. All of the toys were inside, including the speedboat. So he didn't have to look for a playground with a pond, just a playground.

He went downstairs to the hall. The man with the pencil moustache took his key. 'Your kid went out alone,' he said, 'half an hour ago.'

'I know.' Hiller looked at the rack of tourist brochures. 'Have you got a map?'

'Your kid went out alone, and now you want a map?' The man stared at him.

Hiller opened a bus-route. It showed the London parks. He put it in his pocket and turned away.

But the man had noticed his red-rimmed eyes, his shaking hands. 'Wait a minute. We had a bit of a night last night, didn't we?'

'It's nothing.'

'Nothing? I don't know about that.'

'Some people when they wake up,' Hiller said, 'that's the best they're going to feel all day.'

Out on the pavement the day hit him. There was the roar of a compressor from the new hotel, the squeal of a pulley hauling up buckets of cement. And further away the stutter of road-drills. Everything that could be done to change the face of the street was being done.

Ahead there were signs glowing against the grey sky, BROOKS SECRETARIES, MATES. Hiller joined the people hurrying to work. They were girls most of them, small girls with tiny ankles and great high heels like marionettes. Quite ordinary faces were wearing masks, they had huge black eyes and a cold toxic blue to their mouths. In the booming guitars of THE HUNGRY YEARS Hiller vanished among the crowd.

'It was him, I tell you.' Gort turned from the window.

'Well, how was I to know?' the new man said. 'I mean, you said a guy with a young kid.'

'All right. All right.' Gort was angry. He picked up his

15

jacket and went to the door. 'Now you stay here, Sanders. You stay right here by the phone . . . And I don't know if I got much of a chance. There's the bus stop down there, and the tube.'

Hiller got off the bus and went through the Park gates. It was quiet inside, there were black winter trees in the distance, and women walking their dogs. One of them told him the way to the playground.

It was on a slope under the trees. Their trunks were linked together by a catwalk of planks, crudely nailed together and painted in bright circus colours. It was possible to traverse the muddy downslope crookedly, tree by tree, never touching the ground. And on the way there were forts, ramshackle houses, a huge city that had grown up storey by storey, Desperate Dan style. No-one but children, or men with the minds of children, could have built it. And Hiller could only admire. The signs too – NO ADULTS. BROS IS A PUFF. EDDIE SMELLS. ADULTS, KNOCK, KEEP OUT. Hiller kept out.

Then he saw the boy, standing close to a fat boy who was whispering behind his hand. Hiller went up to the high ground by a hut where he would be nearer. BUM, said a sign, DRUGS ARE GOOD. There were European *au pair* girls there, stiff in their good Geneva coats. They looked down at the children, and they cared only about their homes that were far away. DRUGS ARE GOOD. Hiller shivered.

'Come on,' he shouted to the boy.

But he'd climbed away up the branches of a tree, the fat boy leading, cunning on his feet. They started across to the next tree on a narrow plank, fully eight feet from the ground.

'Come on,' Hiller shouted again. He was afraid for the boy. And then, as he looked round at the *au pair* girls and the dripping trees, afraid for himself. There was no protection here. Not if he was being followed.

The boys had reached a wooden platform, fifteen, maybe twenty feet up. From it there was a Commando

16

rope-run, sliding on a wooden block across the clearing. The fat boy unhitched the rope. He made the motions of holding it and jumping out into space. Then he handed it to the boy.

'Oh, Christ.' Hiller started forward, scattering the *au pair* girls.

The boy launched himself high up in the grey day. He'd got the action of the fat boy, the Commando leap, but not the way to grip the rope. He fell, burning his hands, and landed hard on his feet, before crumpling over.

Hiller got to him. 'Are you all right?'

The boy stood up. He moved slowly, hurting, but he could stand. Then he limped away. Hiller didn't want to chase him because of the watching *au pair* girls.

The fat boy came down from the tree. His face was crooked and smiling. 'He didn't do it the way I showed him.'

'No,' Hiller said. 'It wasn't your fault.'

The fat boy went and talked to the boy. Then he turned. 'Does he have to go, Mister?'

'Yes, he does. We're late.'

Hiller started towards them. The fat boy waited, weighing him up. 'You don't want to go, Mister. You should stay here a while. I could fix you up.' He nodded at the *au pair* girls.

Hiller stopped.

'That girl at the end. I know her. It could be fixed up.'

'No.'

'Her bazaars aren't big, but they'll grow. In a few months those bazaars'll be good.'

'Why aren't you at school?' was all Hiller could say.

'I don't go in Thursdays. Thursdays we do Drama.'

Hiller took the boy's hand and led him away.

They came down from the bare trees towards the women walking their dogs. The sound of the traffic got nearer.

'Did you hurt yourself?' Hiller asked.

The boy didn't answer, but he remembered to limp for

the next twenty yards. Then he looked up. 'I s'pose you'll count that as running away? And I don't get my pocket money?'

'We'll see.'

'We'll see. I know what that means.'

They went back through the gates to the traffic, the boy lagging behind on the pavement. 'We agreed on £10.00 for the day, didn't we?'

'£7.50.'

'Not what I remember.'

Hiller didn't answer.

'Not what I remember, Shirley,' the boy said louder. 'I'm right, aren't I, Shirl?'

A man standing by a phone-box looked round at them. Hiller walked by. Sometimes the boy called him Shirley when he was angry.

'All right, Shirl, let's call it £5.00 for the day. How about that, Shirl?'

'We'll see.'

'We'll see, we'll see,' the boy sneered. 'Can't you say anything else?'

They went on in silence. Then they passed a woman at the kerb. She was leaning over a push-chair, her face red as she hit her child. 'Sit straight. Keep your legs up. Stop *wanting* things,' she shouted.

Hiller waited till she was out of earshot. '£5.00,' he said.

Some way behind them on the pavement, Gort was running hard for the phone box.

He pulled himself inside, dialled a number and put money in the slot 'Room II,' he said.

Waiting for the connection, he drummed his fingers on the glass and watched Hiller and the boy walking away up the street.

There was a click. 'Sanders?' Gort said.

'Yes.'

'They're up here on the High Street, both of them. Get here as fast as you can.'

18

'You won't lose them?'

'No.' Gort stared at the two figures. 'Not a chance. He's going towards a pub. He'll go in.'

'But you said he was out of money.'

'He'll go in,' Gort said.

The passage at the side of the pub was dark and tiled. There was a man there, blowing on his hands, and watching over a rack of magazines. Hiller tried to pull the boy quickly past them.

'What's the matter?' The boy hung back.

'Nothing.'

'Why aren't you letting me see?'

'Come on.'

But he was looking back again over his arm. 'They're all part of that thing, aren't they?'

'What thing?'

'The fixing up thing. What that boy was on about in the playground.'

'Don't worry about it.'

'I'm not worried.'

They reached the Public Bar. Hiller stopped. The knot was in his stomach, there was that smell coming through the open door. But he couldn't take the boy inside, he'd never done that. And he couldn't leave him out here, with the magazines.

'None of them are smiling.'

'What?' Hiller turned.

'None of the girls in the pictures are smiling. They usually are, I mean, in pictures.'

Hiller bent down. 'You don't have to worry about them. They're for people who're unhappy, they don't want smiling pictures.'

Quickly he led the boy back past the magazine-seller to the High Street. He reached the corner.

And there was Gort, coming along the pavement towards the alley.

Hiller grabbed the boy back into shadow.

Gort, the hard black Brylcreemed hair, the dark suit, the old-fashioned tie-clip with the chain. All of Hiller's fear returned, he couldn't move.

Behind him, the boy was still looking at the pictures. 'There's *more* to it, isn't there? A lot more than a man putting his thing into a girl's thing? I mean, anybody knows about . . .'

'. . . Get that kid away from here,' the magazine-seller said.

Hiller picked him up and ran. Past the door of the Public, past the dustbins at the end of the alley. Then he came out in a side street, by a church. He couldn't carry the boy any more. He put him down, and held his arms so that he faced him.

'Which is your right hand?'

The boy raised it.

'Now you go down there.' Hiller pointed. 'You go to the right at the end, and then the right again. You'll be out in the wide street. You go over it at the crossing, when the little green man lights up. And you go to the Underground Station.'

'But . . .'

'. . . You get two fifty p tickets.' Hiller handed him the money. 'And then you wait *inside* the barrier, by the ticket collector. You wait for me, and you don't move. Not for anyone except me.'

The boy stared up at him, frightened. Hiller was frightened too. 'Go on,' he said.

He watched the small figure run away down the street, watched him follow his right hand and disappear. Then he turned and ran in the other direction, but slower, trying to lead Gort away.

When he got back to the High Street he saw the crossing in the distance, and the Tube Station on the far side. No sign of the boy. Then he saw Gort, waiting for him on this side, his black suit flapping in the gusts of traffic.

Car horns blared as Hiller ducked across the road. He dodged between them and ran hard, knowing that Gort would have turned towards the noise. He reached the far pavement, the Tube Station was two hundred yards away, and he thought he was going to make it.

Then he saw the second man leaning against a shop window. His leather jacket squeaked as he came away from the glass. He grabbed Hiller and held on to him.

3

It was the room where he'd started out this morning. The room with the case full of toys. And the boy would still be waiting at the Tube Station with two tenpenny tickets. Hiller couldn't think clearly any more.

There were just the two of them. Sanders had brought him back to the hotel alone. He was stretched out on the bed, watching Hiller. Then they both heard the footsteps on the landing. 'Open up.' It was Gort's voice.

Hiller turned away to the window. He saw the new hotel, and the empty lot next to it where they were laying foundations. *Glan-ka*, he heard the sound of the pile-driver. *Glan-ka*. He tried to remember the shape of Gort's clothing, if there was a bulge. If it was going to be a hammer, or a length of lead pipe. He was very afraid of being crippled.

'Turn round,' Gort said. 'Take your jacket off. Put your hands on your head.'

'Look, Gort . . .' Hiller faced him.

'. . . Jacket off. Hands on head.' It wasn't loud, it was advice. Calm advice on the way to lessen pain, from a hospital porter. Gort's own jacket was off, and there was a workman's smell about him. The chewing gum, the dirty shirt cuffs, were a workman's, and Hiller was afraid.

'Stand forward. Up on your toes.'

Sanders moved behind Hiller, pushing him forward until he teetered and nearly fell. Gort pulled his shirt out at the front. All the time he was chewing.

Then suddenly he grunted. The knife came up, a long blade, slicing through his shirt, hissing past his cheek. Hiller lost his balance.

'On your toes. Forward, like I said.'

It was crazy. Sanders pushed him forward again. He nearly overbalanced. Gort chewed on, grunted, and the knife came up again. A needle pain up and across Hiller's stomach. Red on the shirt.

'You don't want to hurt me.'

'That's right.' Gort grunted again. The knife came up.

'You don't want to hurt me. You need me.'

But it went on. Gort's head moving, the smell of his Brylcreem, his workman's sweat, the grunts. And Hiller shaking on his toes, wet dribbling from his mouth as his shirt was cut to pieces, the blood there.

Then it stopped. Gort went to the basin, rinsed the knife and put it away. He looked at his watch and went out.

There was the sound of the phone-bell from the landing.

Sanders stayed in the room. He didn't look at Hiller, he combed his hair.

The phone-bell dinged again. Gort came back. 'It's okay,' he said. 'And I phoned for a taxi. It'll be right round.'

Then the two of them went out.

Hiller didn't understand anything any more. Not even when he pulled on his coat, wrapped it round his blood-stained shirt, and went after them, clattering down the stairs.

They were standing on the pavement, hugging themselves in the cold wind. They didn't look at him, they turned away.

'What is it? What's okay?' He had to shout against the compressor across the street, the beat of the pile-driver. *Glan-ka.*

They didn't hear.

Glan-ka. 'What *is* it?' Hiller shouted.

Then the taxi came. Sanders flagged it down and got in. Gort followed, leaving the door open. Hiller was trembling again. He knew he could go with them or not go, they didn't care. He got in.

'Bond Street,' Gort said to the driver.

They went down Bond Street, dodging the parked Bentleys and the chauffeurs. 'Keep over to the left,' Gort said. 'Slow up now.'

And there at a pavement café, under a giant black and white umbrella, was the boy. He was laughing. And Salto was feeding him ice-cream.

Hiller gave in. 'All right,' he said to Gort.

4

The flat was in a tall Victorian building off a square. Inside it was surprisingly light, but in a bleak white-painted way. Sanders went up the hall and put Hiller's suitcases down by an open door.

'Thank you, dear Heart,' a voice said inside the room. 'That's all we'll be needing from you right now. You'll send in your bill, won't you?'

Hiller knew the voice, Salto's voice. He watched Sanders go back down the hall and let himself out. Then he waited.

Gort motioned him in through the door.

And he saw Salto, tall and thin against the bay window at the end of the room. There was the long black hair which had nothing feminine about it, the wide flat forehead which gave him a brutish cave-man appearance. 'Hi, Hiller.' He came over.

Hiller didn't say anything. He saw that the boy was unharmed. He was playing on the floor with a new toy, an Action Man.

'I bought him an Ackshee Bubber,' Salto said. 'Very butch, with the scar on his cheek and all.' He didn't smile. Humour wasn't part of Salto's make-up. He just used it to blunt his sharp edges. He was twenty-seven.

Hiller shifted uncomfortably. His jacket came open, and Salto saw the blood on his shirt.

'I should get cleaned up,' he said softly. 'I shouldn't let him see you like that.'

Gort took him away down the hall. It was a large flat, but bare. The old Victorian rooms had been stripped, the floors sanded, and the modern furniture seemed to be panicking under the high ceilings. It was dirty too. There were women in Salto's life, Hiller found as he reached the bathroom, but not cleaning women. Women who left in the morning after cups of coffee.

Slowly, painfully, he peeled off his tattered shirt. He didn't look good in the mirror. His belly was criss-crossed with wounds, his face grey and sweating. And as soon as he put on a clean shirt he started to sweat again.

He followed Gort back to the front room. Salto was waiting, standing quite still. There was this control about him. As if there was something inside him he was afraid of, as if he'd schooled himself to take care. It made Hiller nervous.

'Baby,' Salto said to the boy, 'would you go and play in another room? Your daddy and I want to talk business. Long words. Very boring.'

'I like it in here.'

'Take Ackshee Bubber with you. See if you can break something.'

The boy went out.

Salto turned round. 'Sit down,' he said.

Hiller looked about him. The furniture was all knee-high, soft leather or hard polystyrene, nowhere for a man of his age to sit. He chose a chair and sat forward, his belly creasing large between his thighs.

Salto came over with whisky and a bowl of nuts. 'Drinkees? Eatees?' His voice was flat and classless. It was difficult to tell if he'd come up from the East End or down from Public School. He had the regulation Levis and tailored shirt, the pale stubbled face, and the tiredness that worked with certain women. But the rest of him was control.

'Are you sitting comfortably? Right, we'll begin.' He stood facing Hiller. 'Once upon a time there was this guy, whose wife ran off and left him with a kid.'

And put like that, Hiller could almost take it.

'He started boozing, paying for it with bad cheques, got himself in schtuck.' Salto paused. 'But the thing that interested me was that he worked for a company called ILR. Because I'd been looking for a guy who worked there for a long time.'

'If it's the money,' Hiller said.

'If it's the money? Isn't that sweet?' Salto turned to Gort. 'I gave this guy five hundred quid to get a certain article from ILR. There was to be another five hundred when he delivered. But he didn't show. He got scared out of his tiny mind. He got in on the Scotch till it was coming out of his ears. And then he did a very silly thing. He got the sack.'

Hiller waited, not looking at him.

'And you know where the rest of my five hundred went? A nice little holiday in the West Country, cream teas, mystery coach trips,' Salto mimicked a woman's voice, 'and we only had three days of rain . . . Was it three days of rain, by the way?'

Hiller didn't answer.

'But the money had to run out some time, didn't it? And then you ran for the big city, the lights, or maybe you had a friend here.' Salto spread his hands. 'My, my. Right on our doorstep. Didn't you know that, dear Heart? Didn't you know we kept open house?'

Gort moved then, over to the sideboard. He took a glass and tapped it steadily against the shelf.

'We had a little ugly this morning, didn't we?' Salto said.

Gort tapped the glass harder. It broke, leaving a jagged edge.

'And what I want you to do,' Salto said, 'is go back to that company called ILR and collect that certain article.'

'I can't go back there,' Hiller told him, 'not now.'

'Not now. Tomorrow.' Salto made it a fact. 'I mean, they know you there. They'll let you in. You'll just have to think of some excuse.'

'It's not that easy. You . . .'

Gort came towards him with the broken glass.

'We don't want to have a *very* ugly,' Salto said. 'Do we?'

Hiller left it until midnight before he went into the room where the boy was. Because he'd given in. Because they'd let him get in on the Scotch then, a lot of Scotch. And the boy had never seen him like this.

But the boy was awake. He sat up as the key turned on the outside of the door. 'Why're they locking us in?'

Hiller tried to keep the small face still in the spinning darkness. 'Want us to stay here,' he said.

'What?'

Swaying, Hiller made it to his bed. He sat down. 'Don't run away tomorrow. Mean that. Uncle Salto very strong on things like that.'

'But you'll be here?'

'What?

'You'll be here tomorrow?'

Hiller didn't answer.

'You're going away?'

'Only to the place where I work,' Hiller said. 'Be back in the evening.'

There was a long silence.

'You didn't tell me a story.' The boy's voice was low.

'It's too late.'

'Just a short one. Sooty Ann and Mousey Tongue. The Continuing Saga Of Sod's Law.'

The darkness roared round Hiller's head.

Then the boy used a strange word: 'Please.'

And suddenly Hiller saw how he depended on the story. How he was afraid, and had been all along.

'One morning when the sun was high . . .' He picked up any words he came across. '. . . And all the bloodhounds in the neighbourhood . . . were hungover on Rhesus Negative, and saying never again . . .'

5

ILR, Data Division, had been designed to impress Americans. It was on a wooded Buckinghamshire estate, twenty-five miles from London. The new buildings were screened by trees, and the original Tudor house now served as the administration block. Its entrance hall was of dark panelled oak, and there were imported gladioli glowing coldly against the winter's day outside.

The commissionaire was a tall man, straight and grey. He looked down at Hiller as he came in, and he saw past the newly pressed suit to the white face and hurting eyes. 'Didn't expect to see you back here,' he said sourly.

Hiller clutched his forehead. 'When I want your opinion I'll ask for it. Or the head cleaner's come to that.'

The commissionaire stood straighter, pushing out his campaign ribbons. 'What d'you want?' He was looking at Hiller's briefcase.

'I've got an appointment with HG, at twelve.'

'We'll see.' The man walked away and picked up a phone.

Hiller waited. His hangover was bad, but it was helping to keep down his fear. So far.

'You're early.' The commissionaire came back. 'HG'll

see you in ten minutes.'

'That's all right then.' Hiller turned away.

'Where you going?'

'See someone.'

'Like Derek, in the bar?'

And that was exactly what Hiller wanted him to think. He went down the corridor towards the executive restaurant, but then he turned off through a cleaner's door. A flight of scuffed wooden stairs led up past the Accounts Department. It was a route Hiller had used many times, coming back late from the bar.

He crossed over the covered way that led to the new buildings. Oak panelling and gladioli were things of the past. Dust-proof doors opened onto a world of cold strip-lighting, stainless steel, and the humming of machines. He went into a locker room and put on a white coat. Then he clipped on the ILR lapel badge, the blue plastic square he should have handed in when he left. He had to be careful now.

Twice he thought he was in trouble. The first time was when Parry walked by with a group of programmers. The second when Stevenson passed, Stevenson who'd worked on the next bench. But neither man looked round. And then it was easier. He was higher up in the building, the corridors were deserted, and the steel doors hissed open as he approached them with his lapel badge. Then the final door. CLASSIFIED SECURITY LIBRARY. CS AUTHORISED PERSONNEL ONLY. Hiller's badge was good. The door opened.

Heygate sat behind his counter, sweating in the controlled temperature. And Heygate, who was a fortnight behind on his files, a month behind the world, was easy. He didn't even know Hiller had left.

'What can I do for you, Chief?'

'I want to check out a bit of core,' Hiller said. 'I've got an intermittent fault on a channel.'

'Oh, yes?' Heygate sighed.

'It'll have to be a simulation-type job, one that uses a lot of core.'

'Help yourself.' Heygate waved an arm at the steel vaults.

It took Hiller some time to find the tape. And when he did, his hand trembled on the can. It was labelled CHAMPERS, in the tricky bloody way the security people had. Hiller stared at it. He could put it back, go home, and nobody would ask any questions. Except there wasn't any home. Only Salto's flat, with the boy locked in the bedroom.

He put the can under his arm, hiding the label, and went back to Heygate.

'You want me to sign out?'

'What's the use?' Heygate smiled tiredly. 'You won't bother to bring it back.'

'Christ, no.'

Then Hiller was running, down to the Process Department. He'd timed it right, midday, and the European Jobs were in progress. The room was empty under the flickering striplights. Just the whirr and stop of tape channels, the hum of rotary files. And the back-up tape, checking that the right message was being received in Germany, ninety seconds behind. Forty-five seconds to Düsseldorf, and forty-five seconds back.

Hiller found an empty Print-Out, and threaded up the CHAMPERS tape. Then he went round to the front of the machine, undid four screws, and tore through the roll of paper that was the log. No traces, Salto had said. And that was the only point where Hiller agreed with him.

He started the machine. The tape ran past the magnetic head, the paper Print-Out jerked down in concertina folds to the basket below. It would take fourteen minutes to finish. Two minutes down to HG's office, two minutes back, and that meant Hiller would have to stretch his interview out to ten minutes. He sweated at the thought of it.

'You've come to see me about a reference?' HG couldn't believe it.

'That's right.' Hiller stared across the desk at the man with the boy's head. It was the straight parting and the quiff. HG couldn't look like a man, even with the two initials and the tight black suit that were regulation in the Admin. building.

'It's going to be difficult,' he said. 'I mean, I'm quite prepared to write you a reference. Nobody wants to see you go down.'

The thin mouth said the opposite. Hiller had to go down, he had to be seen to go down. That was why he'd been given the appointment this morning.

For a moment he felt like giving up and walking out. But he made himself smile. There were eight minutes left before he could get back to the Print-Out machine.

'You see, we have the circumstances of your sacking.' HG frowned at the open file in front of him.

Circumstances, if you could call five pints of Worthington circumstances. It was the bad time when Hiller had been trying to stick to beer in the middle of the day, and the final lunchtime session which had ended at 3 pm. . .

HG wanted to see him. And he knew about the beer. He kept Hiller waiting twenty-five minutes in the outer room. On purpose. Hiller crossed and re-crossed his legs. Through the open door, the girls in the typing pool giggled. It was somehow very important not to walk back past them to the Gents. Finally – crazily in his agony – he decided on the waste paper basket. He pushed it along the bench until he was hidden from view. Then, when he was halfway through, the bell rang, and the girls filed past the door on their way to tea.

'Circumstances which can't be dismissed lightly,' HG said at last.

'I was just caught short.'

'You gave offence. And there were other times you gave offence in those last few months. I mean, you'd always done a certain amount of drinking. But in the end it got out of hand, it got insane.' HG looked at the file again. 'The night when you were racing to this pub before it closed. You hit a tree, and the Law was involved. You gave a long statement to the constable. Three pages, which included your theories on,' he blinked at the words, 'Wagner's Opera, Tristan.'

Hiller didn't say anything.

'And in the end you refused to sign the statement. You threw the constable's torch into a pond.' He frowned. 'You, a man with a High Security clearance.'

'You know how it can be,' Hiller said, 'sometimes.'

'I don't. I'm afraid I don't.'

That thin mouth again. Hiller looked at his watch. There were six minutes left.

'But my work's always been good, hasn't it?' he asked.

'Oh, no doubt about that.'

'Well, then?'

'It's not enough. Not in these days, when Company loyalty counts for so much.'

My backside, Hiller thought. 'You're right,' he said.

'Towards the end of your time here, you'd never work late. You wouldn't go on any of the courses with the others, Seattle or Copenhagen. In fact, you refused to go.'

Hiller didn't answer. He didn't want to go into that.

'Well?'

'I couldn't leave home at that time,' he said finally. 'There were problems.'

'Problems, at home.' HG chewed on a nail.

Hiller knew he should get out, right now. But there were still five minutes left.

'A modern forward-looking Company has to glance at its employee's homelife.' HG shrugged. 'Just glance. Even I don't escape the net.'

HG's home life, Hiller thought. One gin in the evening, a frozen pizza and he's tired. Mrs HG watching 'Come Dancing.' Forty yards of tulle.

'And especially in this case, when your home-life was brought forcibly to our attention.' HG held up a photocopy. 'Solicitor's letter. Sent to us because they couldn't get satisfaction from you . . . A coal bill for £287? How on

31

earth did that happen?'

'This coalman, he let it go on for a long time. There was a place where I used to get him 90 proof rum. He understood that sort of thing.'

HG didn't. He frowned. 'But you were spending a great deal of money elsewhere. The gramophone you bought at discount through the company.'

'Parts of a gramophone,' Hiller corrected him. 'I built the damn thing myself.'

'Those parts cost over £800. I mean, the speakers alone were designed to fill a lecture-hall.'

'They are good, though.'

'And six hundred LP records?'

Hiller was startled. 'Where d'you hear that?'

'You talked about your collection to people here.'

'I *mentioned* it to a couple of people. Christ.'

'And your wife doesn't even like Classical music.'

'I suppose I *mentioned* that too.' Hiller was angry. But he kept it down. There were only four minutes left. 'She had her own interests, I had mine,' he said. 'Simple as that.'

'And then she became ill.' HG made a weak effort at sympathy.

Hiller stared at him. 'How d'you know?'

'It's the sort of thing one would talk about, isn't it?'

Never. She hadn't been ill, she'd been out. And then there'd been the day when she hadn't come back. But he'd never talked about that to anyone. Ever.

'. . . Only the Personnel Manager here,' HG was saying. 'I'm only trying to find the circumstances behind a troubled employee.'

'That's good,' Hiller said.

'In my experience, 99% of these troubles stem from the home.'

Hiller opened his mouth. Then he decided to let it go. There were just over three minutes left.

'You rented your house.' HG turned a page in the file. 'And you didn't look after it. The lawns not cut or anything.'

'I did get a goat once,' Hiller said tiredly. 'It ran away.'

'A rented house is never looked after,' HG insisted. 'No incentive . . . And just look at you, all the time you were frittering your money away on gramophone records.'

'Frittering? Six-hundred records?'

'But you see, you had nothing behind you. No mortgage. No bricks and mortar.' HG folded his hands. 'And that's just the sort of insecurity that eats into a woman. No home to call her own.'

Hiller's head came up.

Just you leave it, he thought. Leave it alone.

But HG couldn't. All the mortgage rose up in him, all the evenings he'd spent painting bedrooms with his wife. 'As I understand it, she didn't do a great deal of housework. She let the place get dirty. And the child . . .'

'. . . Leave it.' Hiller was suddenly on his feet.

HG was startled.

'It doesn't matter that you've got it all wrong,' Hiller started quietly. 'Doesn't even matter that you wouldn't understand it anyway.'

'What d'you mean?'

'It was Stevenson, wasn't it? He told you all this. He came to supper, just the one time.'

'I don't want you to think we rely on gossip.'

'You just have to be one of your shiny-suited men,' Hiller said bitterly. 'You have to be part of the fifth-column and pass on all the talk. Have to keep your nose clean at home, switch on the television anytime a row looms up. Because you can't have rows, not real ones, when you're all bandaged up with mortgages and bloody ducks on the wall.' He was standing over HG now. 'My God, you sit it out until that great day finally comes, when you get your Rover Tinear Cruoris, your four-bedroomed fake Georgian, and you can trade in your wife for a St Bernard dog.'

'St Bernard?' HG was lost.

Hiller backed away. He was snarling, helpless. He couldn't even get this right.

'You don't want a reference, I take it?' HG asked finally.

'Up you,' Hiller said. He walked out.

The tape was finished. Hiller scooped up the paper Print-Out and stuffed it in his briefcase. Then he ran.

He ran to the Classified Library, passed Heygate at his desk, and dropped the CHAMPERS tape into its rack.

'Can't be pub-closing, can it?' Heygate watched him come back.

He ran down to the locker room, took off the white coat, and slipped his blue lapel badge into his front pocket.

Then he went down to the entrance hall.

'What's your hurry?' The commissionaire barred his path.

Hiller shook his head, panting.

'What you got in that briefcase?'

'Coshes,' Hiller said.

'Oh, yes?' The commissionaire moved in until his medal ribbons were against Hiller's face.

'Just as well we had you on our side, wasn't it?' Hiller said.

But he shouldn't have said that. The man stared down at him and saw the lapel badge in his front pocket.

'You were meant to hand that in when you left. You know that.'

'I didn't know I still had it.'

'Then I'd better take it from you, hadn't I?'

Hiller told himself it didn't matter, it wouldn't be remembered. He was free of ILR now, free of Salto, it was all over. He only had to hand over the Print-Out, pick up £500, and pass Go.

6

Salto let him in. He took the briefcase without a word. Hiller went on to the bedroom.

And he was worried. He saw the Action Man on the floor, its arms and legs torn off.

Then he saw Gort sitting on the bed, crumpled up in his dark suit. 'Bloody kid,' he said.

But it was Gort who was bloody. A thin scar ran down the back of his hand. The boy was unmarked, sitting high up on top of the wardrobe.

'Halle-*lu*-jah for *Je*-sus who *died* up a *tree*,' he sang.

'You all right up there?' Hiller asked.

The boy nodded.

'Get your things together then. We're going.'

He stopped singing. 'Where to?'

'Where d'you want to go?'

'Bognor sounds nice. It's a nice sound.'

'It's not far enough away.'

'Couldn't we make a Bognor further away?'

'You're right,' Hiller said. He turned to find the suit-cases.

Then he stopped. Salto was out in the hall. He had the Print-Out with him, and there was something about the way he was standing.

Hiller waited, his smile going. He could feel the £500 getting further away.

'It's just figures, isn't it?' Salto said.

'What did you expect?'

'Something I could read.'

'It's only a straight Print-Out,' Hiller said. 'An Edit

would have left traces. It would've meant getting hold of the Job Control Cards, calling down a specific programme, having a talk-session with the Console.'

'And I'm telling you in English, this isn't any use to me.'

'Now there's a thing.' Hiller was angry.

'Getting gutty all of a sudden, aren't we, dear Heart?' Salto didn't raise his voice, didn't seem to move quickly, he just had Hiller tight against the wall.

And Hiller was frightened as he stared up at the black stubble, the dark shadows under the eyes. Salto hadn't slept last night, he didn't know when he slept. There was just this cold hard purpose about him.

'All right.' Hiller nodded, and Salto let him go. 'All right, I've got an ILR code-book in my briefcase. With that, and any decent-sized computer, you could get what you want in a couple of hours.'

'Another computer?' Salto was wary.

'There are bureaus,' Hiller said. 'Small firms, who rent out time.'

'But they're going to keep records?'

'Of course.'

'No.' Salto shook his head. 'Nobody but us knows we've got hold of this. It's not leaving here.'

'Look, this is Graded stuff' Hiller pointed at the Print-Out. 'And what that means is, before you even get to the ILR code, there's a High Security code to break. And that's the bastard. It's a one-off, never used before or since. I don't even know the form of it, the fields, the boundaries, whether it's hexa or straight decimal.'

'You must be trying to tell me something,' Salto said. 'All I want to know is, can you crack it without a machine?'

'Oh, it's possible.' Hiller ran a hand through his hair. He was angry, a scientist confronted by a layman. 'Christ, anything's possible, given enough time.'

'You've got a week.' Salto turned away. 'That's if you want that five hundred quid.'

'Just like that? Cold? With nothing to go on?' Hiller

went after him. 'You have to key me in with something. Some words or headings that might repeat.'

Salto stopped then. 'Three words that might be there quite a lot,' he said, 'are National General, and Bank.'

7

Hiller was back where he'd started, in the front room. And he was angry, he could see more of it now, the senseless abuse. There was the huge television set mounted in a steel globe. There were the clusters of spotlights, the goat-skin rugs, Italian leather chairs, all new and expensive. But what was senseless was the way they'd been treated. The cigarette burns, the tears in the leather, the drink-stains and scratches. And out in the shadows, the rows of empty wine bottles in the dust. It was like a stand at an exhibition, on the last day.

Salto and Gort sat watching him. The boy was locked in his room. Everything was as it was before.

Except for the Print-Out, a concertina of white paper on the table.

'Well, dear Heart?'

'Well, what?' Hiller stared at it. 'D'you have any idea how much information you've got there? You lay the whole thing out and it's sixty feet long.'

'Meaning, you have to know more?'

Hiller nodded.

'Don't tell him anything,' Gort said.

'He'll know in the end, won't he, Gorty? Once he cracks that thing, it'll all be there, staring at him.'

Gort hadn't thought about that.

Salto went over to the window and looked out at the dusk. When he turned back, he moved his whole body round like a man with a stiff neck. The control was there, all the time.

'Your big bank,' he said, 'how many times d'you reckon it's been done? Broken into, broken out of, and gone away?'

'I don't know,' Hiller said. He didn't want to know.

'I'm not talking about the daylight bit, the heavy boys camping around with shotguns. I mean the smart bit, the break-in at night. How many times?'

Hiller shook his head.

'It hasn't been done,' Salto said.

'Is that a fact?'

'Oh, come on, Hearty. You read the *News of the World*. So you say to me, what about the walkie-talkie raid over at Baker Street?. . . And I say to you, that was more than ten years ago. Because it was just ten years ago when the Big Five banks got it all together. They went computerized, and they called in the Security experts. And I do mean experts.' He came towards Hiller. 'All that stuff you've seen on TV. . . . alarm-bells, wired floors, light beams you have to step over . . . that's as out of date as Stephenson's Rocket.'

Salto paused. He got a tin of small cigars from his jeans pocket and lit one. 'Little story,' he said. 'Are we sitting comfortably? Right, we'll begin.'

'For Christ's sake.' Hiller said.

'Once upon a time,' Salto ignored him, 'about eighteen months ago, I was driving through the town of Smethington. You know it?'

'No.'

'Used to be a railway town of character. That was before the working-classes tasted scampi. Now it's little boxes and traffic-jams . . . Anyway I was in the usual snarl-up, stuck at the traffic-lights. And over the road, I saw two men with pickaxes knocking a hole in the wall of the National General Bank . . . So what did I do? I parked the car and went in. "Don't want to bother you, Harold," I said to the cashier, "but there are these two men knocking a hole in the wall". . . "That's all right," he said. "They're installing the new air-conditioning."' Salto's arms fell to his sides. 'Now I only had to look around to see the place had only been painted a month. And I knew the National General Bank, Smethington wasn't stupid enough to redecorate *before* they'd put in air-conditioning. So I went back to the car, and I spent the rest of the day driving around.'

Salto held his cigar out staring at the end. 'And I saw the promised bleeding land. I saw the new building-work going on, factories and estates, all paying wages in cash. I saw the estates already built, and the banks they had out there with their cashpoints. I saw the new Sainsbury's and the Hypermarket. Taking in cash. *Cash.* You could hear the sound of the tills a quarter of a mile away . . . So you see, dear Heart, I began to get an idea why the National General Bank, Smethington was installing air-conditioning a month after it'd been painted.'

Hiller stared at him.

'I drove back into town, and clocked those two work-men outside the bank again. Then I waited for opening time, and I went round the pubs. I found those two kiddies, Irish, both of them. And it was Wednesday night. You couldn't ask for more.' He grinned. 'They drank all I could pour down them, and they told me the National General Bank, Smethington, was being up-graded. There were grades to National General Banks, you see. New wiring was going in, new machinery, and it all had to be handled very carefully. All part of a very so-phis-ti-cated,' he made it Irish, 'security system, from Sanger's. And dear God, it had all been worked out by computers.'

And Hiller began to understand.

'Sanger's deal with ILR, your people. I found out there was a reel of tape. And it only took an afternoon with some computer whizz-kid to find out what the goodies would be on that reel of tape . . . Simulation-type programme. Set up to deal with. . . .' He swung round on Hiller.

39

'. . . Write it. Bloody write it down.'

Hiller found some paper, uncapped his pen.

'Simulation-type programme,' Salto repeated. 'To deal with the increasing amounts of cash being handled. Problems of transporting that cash. Problems of security . . . Branch number of every National General Bank in the country. Predicted cash-flow, in and out, for each of those branches on given dates, say every Wednesday of November 1987, November 1988, 89, 90, and so on. Wednesday being the day before wage packets are made up.'

Hiller was writing quickly.

'The grading of banks as per their predicted cash-flow, High Security down to Low. The cost of the various security systems, the cost of installing them. A Cost-Efficiency Programme, in fact. How much money you're going to have in your bank, and how much it's worth spending on protecting it.' Salto paused. 'That's all I can think of at the moment.'

'It could be enough,' Hiller said, 'if I get lucky.'

'Lucky? This is the luckiest thing you ever heard of,' Salto said quietly. 'We only know exactly how much cash is waiting in any bank in the country. We only know exactly what alarm systems will be waiting for us. And somewhere there just has to be the right bank, the one that . . .'

'. . . Shut it up,' Gort said.

'You're right, Gorty, aren't you?' Salto sat down.

There was silence then. Just the sound of Salto's fingers tapping on his cigar. Hiller didn't look up. Both men were watching him.

'I take it,' he said finally, 'we're going to be here some time, the boy and I.'

'For the duration.' Salto nodded. 'Until it's over.'

'I don't mind for me.' Hiller looked round at the stale, smoke-filled room, then at the girlie magazine in Gort's hands. 'But it's not right for the boy.'

'Oh, yes?' Gort saw where he was looking.

'I mean it,' Hiller said. But he couldn't mean it.

Because with his papers clutched in his hand, his pipe bubbling in his mouth, he was like some middle-aged schoolteacher.

'The sooner you get working on that thing, the sooner we'll all be through,' Salto said. 'And then we can all talk about leaving.'

'Sod's Law.' Hiller's hands shook as he put the Print-Out under his arm. He took it away.

8

Next morning he had the top sheets of the Print-Out spread out in his bedroom. He stared at the first two blocks of characters, and then counted them. They were bastards. The first had 920 characters, the second 960.

He tried to keep it simple. The second block, the normal data block, could have various factors. 960 could be 10 records of 96 characters, 8 records of 120, 12 records of 80, and so on.

But the first block had an 80 character header-record. Therefore it could contain n-I data records, where n was the number of records per block. The factor.

920 in the first block. Subtract 80. Answer 840.

$$\frac{840}{n-1} = \frac{960}{n} \qquad \text{Answer} \quad n = 120.$$

The factor could be 8 records of 120 characters.

Could be. If it was that simple.

Or it could be something else.

In the front room Gort arranged his jacket on a chair and went over to the television. It almost seemed wrong when the huge steel globe came up with Ludlow Races. Gort sat down and folded his *Daily Mirror* in a tight square around the racing section. Then he made bets, his pencil shiny where it ran through his Brylcreemed hair.

The boy's hair was dull and spikey where he'd slept on it. He stood in the bay window and looked out at the day. No breath of it came into the room, the window was closed, double-locked, as it had been for three days now. The boy was pale. Moodily he sat down and felt in his pockets.

Gort swung round at the scrape of a match. 'Where d'you get that fag? Come on, give it here.'

The boy took one more drag and handed it over.

'You got any more?'

'No.'

'Give us those others. And the matches.'

'All right then.'

'I catch you smoking again, and you'll get a good hiding.'

'All right,' the boy said. 'All right, Shirley.'

'And for Jesus' sake, stop calling me Shirley.'

Gort went back to the races, and lost steadily.

The boy played with his toys, the fire engine, and the Schuco racing car.

He wound up the car, and set it so that it ran in circles out to the centre of the room. He followed it, crouching low, and making car-noises. Then he straightened. He was blocking Gort's view of the television. And he knew it.

Gort swore under his breath. He went over to the sideboard and opened a bottle of light ale. When he came back, he kicked his chair into a new position.

The boy crawled on after the car. Gort shifted his chair again. The boy crawled on again.

Suddenly Gort raised his hand and smashed the beer-bottle on the table. 'Nobody moves!'

The boy looked from Gort to the shellburst of beer and broken glass. With admiration.

In the bedroom Hiller was still trying the blocking-factor, 8 records of 120 characters per record.

He skimmed through the ones he'd marked off. He saw that a lot of them were only using 104 out of 120 characters. The rest could be fill-characters, to pad out a short record size.

Could be.

By the time he found out he was wrong, he suddenly looked up and found it was evening.

The only light in the front room came from the television set. But Gort, a hard outline in his black suit, wasn't watching it. His mouth was working crazily on his gum, almost out of control.

The boy was out among the empty bottles. He had one of them in his hand, and he was tapping it steadily against the door.

'You want to go out?' Gort shouted. 'Out to the toilet for the fifty-seventh time?'

'No.'

'No what?'

The boy watched him steadily.

'No what?' Gort asked louder.

'No arseholes.' The boy ran, to the corner where the shadows were deepest.

Gort went after him. He took off his watch, then he swung back his hand.

'No sky,' the boy shouted. 'No bulldozer. No gumboot.'

'*Say* it.' Gort's hand went further back.

'No . . . No thank you.'

'You just watch your language.' Gort went back to his chair.

And then, for Hiller in the bedroom, it always seemed to be evening. He didn't know how long he'd been working, three days, four days. He only knew the characters were blurring on the page. And they wouldn't come right.

He'd gone through four different blocking factors. He'd tried conversions in certain fields, tried to decide what were values and what were codes, tried to find patterns and play around with them.

But nothing would come.

He stood up and looked round at the smoke in the room. He was tired, he'd burned up a lot of what was inside him. It showed in his eyes, in the sour mouth that was dragged down by his pipe. But he wasn't beaten, there was a bulldog quality to the man. Because figures, or the logic of figures, he understood. And if the human brain couldn't beat them, then there were machines that could. He went to find Salto.

Salto was sprawled out on his bed. He listened for a moment, then he shook his head. 'No computer bureau,' he said. 'I told you that before.'

'All right.' Hiller stood there puffing at his pipe.

'All right, what?'

'It can't be done.'

Salto sat up quickly, on one elbow.

'Ask anyone. Ask the head Data Processor at ILR.' Hiller shrugged. 'As far as I can see, it's a shifting code, with various blocking factors. The only way to break it is to play around on a terminal in a computer bureau.'

'You mean that?'

Hiller didn't answer.

'These bureaus?' Salto asked finally. 'What sort of places are they?'

'There are maybe fifty of them in London. They work non-stop, nine-to-five, on any jobs that come in. This'll just get lost in the pile.'

'But you said they kept records?'

'What of, for God's sake? I can't make head or tail of this, so who else is going to?'

'You'll be getting answers, won't you?' Salto said quickly. 'In this bureau?'

'I'll be getting them in ILR code,' Hiller said. 'And there are only twenty-five copies of the ILR code book in the country.'

Salto put his head on one side. 'You're not getting clever with me, are you, dear Heart? I'd hate to think you were

44

doing that.'

'How many days have I been working now?' Hiller asked. 'Four? Five? And I've got nowhere. Complete washout.'

Salto stared at him. He saw the exhaustion on his face, and the truth that came with exhaustion. 'All right, it's the bureau,' he said. 'If there's no other way.'

'There isn't.' Hiller went to the door.

Then they both heard it.

The boy's cry from the front room.

Hiller got there first. He pulled open the door. And he stood there, afraid.

Gort had his jacket off, his sleeves rolled up. There was that smell about him Hiller remembered from the Earl's Court room.

The boy was crouching, small and bony with his anger, in the corner.

'What about your toys?' Gort was shouting.

'I'm bored of them.'

'What about that motor boat you were playing with yesterday?'

'In that stupid little bath?'

'What about the television then?' Gort pointed. 'I let you stay up last night, didn't I? Right till the wrestling?'

The boy got up suddenly. He went over to the gleaming metal television and put his foot through the screen.

Salto came past Hiller. 'He doesn't like television any more,' he said calmly.

And for that brief moment Hiller admired Salto and his control.

Then he saw Gort turning for his jacket. Saw him go for the boy, knife in hand.

It took both Hiller and Salto to keep him off. Then they swung round. The door was open. And the front door. The boy had gone.

'I'll find him,' Hiller said. 'Will you let me do that? It's the only way.'

Salto went with him, carrying an A to Z Guide. The streets outside the flat were grey, getting towards evening, and the first two playgrounds they tried were empty. Then Hiller remembered the one in the Park, where he'd found the boy that first morning.

It was dusk when they got there. The trees were dark, merging with the sky. The boy was holding onto a tyre on a rope. He was alone in the playground. The lights of real peoples' houses were in the distance, and he was crying.

Hiller made Salto keep back. He went to the boy and sat him on his knee. He pressed the thin bones of his back, and he spoke out of the side of his mouth like a ventriloquist: 'Gred and gutter. Gred and gutter.'

Sober, it was one of the few jokes he had for the boy. But now it wasn't enough. Clumsily Hiller bent down and kissed him. He caught the stale smell of the front room on his hair.

'I'll kill him,' the boy said. 'I'll kill that man.'

'You mustn't say things like that.'

'I was saying things like that before you were born.'

And he meant it. Hiller understood that.

They took him to Jo Lyons for fish and chips. They took him to a cartoon show. Then they took him back to the flat.

'I won't be responsible,' Gort said, 'not any more.'

'We have to find someone.' Hiller turned to Salto. 'It has to be a woman.'

But it was Gort who found her. He wouldn't have

anything to do with Salto's Sloane Square tarts, he said they needed someone they could trust. He rang a woman called Pauline. And an hour later he took Hiller round to meet her.

Pauline lived in a block of flats that came from the Odeon period. It had windows that wrapped round the corners, and metal ribs that showed through the cement. Once it had been respectable. But not now. Pauline was running a film show.

'Come on through,' she said. 'We need to fill the place up. It's a bit slow tonight.'

And it was slow. In the long dim lounge there were only two punters, as she called them. They were both men in their forties, with a golf club heartiness much the worse for drink. There was a young man in jeans working the projector, there was another girl, and there was Pauline behind the bar.

She had bright red lips she left on cigarettes, and a dress that showed large slack breasts. They quivered as she coughed, low and discreetly, behind jewelled hands.

Gort talked to her. Then he came over to Hiller with a whisky. 'She's not sure if she can help out,' he said. 'But she's the one to ask. She's had two kids of her own.'

Hiller turned away. He was uneasy. He'd met women like Pauline before. Not with a video show, but with a flat like this, one that somebody knew about after closing time. The smell of drink-stained carpets, of scent fighting fried food. The smell that people knew who didn't want to go home.

He looked at the video. There was a title – 'When Her Man Goes Away.' Then a black girl sitting on a bed. She had a man's shirt next to her, and the way she was stroking it showed that she wanted him back. Hiller was strangely shocked by her beauty, by her long slim hands. He turned away to the bar as one of the punters came over. He was slackfaced and slow.

'Another one, Ronald?' Pauline asked.

The man didn't look up. He wasn't using his real name.

Pauline knew this, was used to this. 'Another one, handsome?' she asked again.

He nodded. 'We were in this pub tonight.'

'Were you, then?'

'Don't know where it was,' he said. Then, greatly daring: 'There was this dwarf in there, in the Gents.'

'Is that right?'

'I didn't see him, he was so small. I nearly went in his ear.' The man's face didn't go with his daring. He was a commuter, talking dirty to a woman for the first time.

And she let him. 'Oh, yes?'

'I told him I was sorry. I told him there was a Ladies, a Gents. Should've been a Dwarfs too.'

'Course there should.' She and Gort stood there coldly, not moving, but smiling whenever the man looked. They were giving him only what he paid for.

Hiller moved away. On the screen the black girl was under a shower with the shirt. Her beauty had gone, there was only her skill now. And it was skill, a cold hard hunger on her face. Hiller felt uncomfortable. But as he looked around, no-one else was affected.

Then he saw someone who was.

The second girl, the one behind the sofa, was leaning forward, her knuckles white on the cushions. There was a tiny hiss as she breathed in. And the other punter, sitting below her, heard it. He reached out for her hand.

She swung round. It was a sudden shock as she switched off and pushed him away. Hiller couldn't explain it, but it was a pure thing he'd seen. He watched her now, standing alone, guarding herself.

He took Gort on one side. 'Who is she?'

'That one? Anna?' Gort's mouth was turned down. 'She's dikey.'

Pauline heard. 'That's enough,' she said. 'You're all the same, you men. If she won't play, she has to be dikey.'

'She was on the game.' Gort shrugged. 'What you'd call the big game. South Africa and the Bahamas. Where the money is.'

'The money's gone now.'. Pauline lowered her voice. 'She helps out here sometimes, with drinks and things. She's shut the other thing off, like it was a watertight compartment. She's got this five-year-old girl, devotes all her time to her. It's something to admire.'

Hiller still watched her, the girl in the plain grey dress that hid her body. The face without make-up, the dark unwashed hair.

'D'you think she'd come in and look after the boy?' he asked suddenly.

'She needs the money,' Pauline said.

10

She moved into Salto's flat the next day. She had two suitcases, a radio, and a little girl called Mo. The girl sat quietly while her mother took over the spare bedroom next to Hiller's room. She swept it, scrubbed it, and all the time she kept the radio at her side as though she needed a wall of sound around her.

From the beginning she made it plain she was a separate person, entirely self-contained. She still hid her body, in loose trousers and sweater. And she was older than Hiller had thought, maybe thirty, and too thin. She wasn't beautiful, her face was long and hard. It was difficult to connect her with the big game Gort had mentioned. She wore no make-up, she was strangely neutral, like a fashion model walking from one job to another, her face and hair in her handbag, and no expression for the journey in between.

The boy she treated as a separate person too, and he respected that. He watched Mo, the little girl. Where her mother was drab, Mo was brightly dressed, with ribbons in her hair. And it was blonde hair, thin as gold foil, show-ing the shape of her head. All of Mo was fragile. The finger that picked her stub nose with concentration, the pale rounded forehead and huge eyes. She had a doll called Biddy Bandy and a doll called G.D.

'G.D.'s hat keep falling off,' she said.

The boy nodded, keeping his distance.

'Bib-ib,' she made the noise of a car horn and came past him.

He followed her into the kitchen.

'Can I put my apron on? Can I play with water?' Hiller heard her ask.

And it was there in the kitchen, where a moment later he saw her bow her head and lift the hair from her small white neck. And where her mother bent to tie the apron around her. It was there Hiller knew he could leave them with the boy.

He walked into his bedroom, put the Print-Out in his briefcase, and went out to find a computer bureau.

It was early evening when he came back. He laid out a long grey sheet of paper in the front room, the Edit. He worked on a section with his code book. Then he wrote down a sentence.

Salto came over and looked at it.

'Good on you,' he said softly. He turned to Gort. Both men were still.

Hiller stared at them, at their faces. Then he put down his pen.

'Aren't you going to do any more?' Salto asked.

'I need a cup of coffee,' Hiller said, 'in the kitchen.'

But he didn't go to the kitchen. He went to his room, to the bottle of whisky he had hidden in the wardrobe. He sat in the darkness and he drank two, then three glasses with-out stopping.

Because suddenly it had come home to him.

It wasn't a mathematical problem any more, not char-acters per record, groupings of data.

50

It was 703–74–351. NATIONAL GENERAL BANK LTD., 48
CHURCH ST., WALEHAM, BERKS.

11

'Hiller baby.' They were calling him from the front room.

He didn't move. He was well into his fifth glass now, and he didn't care.

'Hiller baby.' They came for him. He was crouching in the angle of the wardrobe door. They saw the half-empty bottle, his soft whisky mouth.

Gort knew what to do about it, and he was rough. He hauled Hiller away to the bathroom and got the liquor out of him. Then he washed his hands, and took him back to Salto.

'Now you stay right here where we can see you, and you finish this thing.' Salto held the Edit out towards him. 'I want banks, branch numbers, addresses, and the details below.'

'Five hundred times, I must rob the National General Bank,' Hiller said.

'You want trouble?'

'Up you.'

Gort took off his watch and smacked him around. Hiller didn't feel it at first, but then it began to get through.

'All right,' he said. 'All right.'

They poured coffee down him. They sat him down and spread the Edit out on the floor. And gradually he was able to see the columns of black figures without them crawling around.

'Just get to work, dear Heart.' Salto stood over him. 'No more nasty little scenes.'

Hiller's mouth was split open, it throbbed. 'You don't

have to worry,' he said. 'I just want to get shot of the whole bloody lunatic thing.'

And that's all it was now, lunacy. A sheet of grey paper that stretched clear across the room, 35 feet of National General Banks. It was going to take a long time to de-code. Tonight, and most of tomorrow.

Salto took the first sheet as Hiller finished it. He stared at it a long time, his face strange.

'It's only the whole thing, the works,' he said quietly. 'Security Rating, Cash Deliveries, and the whole damn Alarm System.'

'That's the Alarm System? There?' Gort asked. 'What's it all mean?'

'I don't know.' Salto shook his head. 'But just look at the cash they've got in there.'

'Jesus. My sweet Jesus.' Gort whistled.

Salto took the sheet of paper away. He squatted down in the corner by the phone. And for some time he sat quite still, staring straight ahead, a dark figure in dirty jeans, five days of growth on his jaw. Then he picked up the phone and went to work.

He started small.

'Maxie? Yes, it's me. And you're right, it's money. . . . Only £750. . . . Look, I wouldn't be ringing you up and asking if I wasn't desperate. There's this thing I've been chasing a long time now, and it's left me skint. I haven't even got the price of a Sunday joint.' He made the motions of smoking.

Maxie was loud and angry at the other end.

Salto was calm. 'All righty. If you want to get your big boots on and get felt all over the borough, that's fine by me. . . . I keep telling you, there's this deal I'm setting up, these people who've been waiting on me a week now. I've got to go out and start buying them forty quid dinners in the West End. Business people. You know how they are. . .'

Quietly, his voice soft, his eyes hard, Salto worked his

way towards £750.

And he got there. Because an hour later the doorbell rang, and a roll of notes was delivered. Salto counted them, and left the room.

When he came back, he was a different man. He was shaved, wearing a dark suit, and a collar and tie.

He saw Hiller's surprise. 'What did you expect, dear Heart? A job like this, it isn't lugging a brick through a window and running away with a sack marked Swag. Not any more. Nowadays you have to start out by attracting investment.'

'Investment?' Hiller stared at him.

'Some of the people running around in striped trousers,' Salto shrugged, 'you just wouldn't believe.'

It was late, after midnight, when he got back from the dinner in the West End. He stood over Hiller a moment, saw he was a quarter way through the Edit, then he went on to Gort. His voice was high and full of wine:

'Well, I got there in the end. Talked to the man himself. The Broker.'

'And he's coming across?' Gort asked.

'He is. Getting together a Consortium, no less. All the schmeer.'

'What's a Consortium?'

'A group of businessmen. It's too big for the Broker himself to handle. So he's getting the others in. They'll come up with the Front Money.'

'When will you know for sure?'

'A couple of days. He wants it all done properly, of course. A budget, schedules, and cut-off points. I'm talking to him again Friday.'

'And there's nothing else he wants?'

'He's coming it a bit with the interest rates,' Salto said. 'But what we've got to deliver . . . hot money . . . is good news right now. All those floating currencies in Europe.'

'How much will he take then?'

'Anything we can give him, up to fifteen mill.'

'And get it away?'

Salto nodded. 'He'll pay us in Deutschmarks or Swiss Francs, lodged abroad.'

'Swiss Francs are the usual, aren't they?' Gort said.

'I reckon so. I mean, Germany's good. I like the way the Germans do things. But Switzerland's safer.'

Gort put a new piece of gum in his mouth. He chewed for a moment. 'How much Front Money's he good for?' he asked then.

'He was talking about letting us have fifty grand. Maybe I could push it up to sixty-five.'

'You'll need all of that, with the Team you'll be wanting on this job.' Gort counted on his fingers: 'A good Bellman, the best. A good Peterman. Then there's the Stoppo Driver and the rest.'

'Who's the best Bellman nowadays?' Salto asked.

'Coppens. That's what I hear, anyway.'

'He was talking about letting us have fifty grand. Maybe for Coppens?' He grinned. 'Black tarts, white tarts, two or three at a time?'

Gort didn't answer.

'What's the matter?'

'Nothing.'

'Coppens and his sort are the old style, is that it? They don't like the new style like me?'

'They don't like amateurs,' Gort said suddenly. 'You're good at the business side, I'll give you that. And you plan things out very thorough. It's just when you start using words like Bellman and Peterman. Like you learned them off a set of frigging gramophone records.'

'Listen, Gort, I pay you.' Salto was angry.

'And I don't know how long I'll be taking your money. Not when the big boys come in.'

'Well, I'll tell you. One thing those big boys haven't got is a list of banks as long as your bloody arm. They couldn't get hold of that in a hundred . . .'

But Gort had gone, out of the door.

Hiller didn't look up from his work as Salto came over.

'You heard all that, I suppose?'

'What?'

'Oh, for Christ's sake, you heard.'

Hiller nodded.

'I don't want you to get the wrong idea. I've made money. I've got money put away.' Salto stood quite still. The control was still there, keeping his anger down. 'It's just that I'm making my Bentley now. And I'm not making it in property, or on the money market. I'm making it with people like Gort. I choose to do that.'

'It's your affair.'

'Yes, it is. But I'll tell you. . . .'

Hiller was uneasy. He didn't know why Salto had to explain.

'There was this time when I was working for a guy in the City,' Salto said. 'His big killing was Government stocks, Funding Six-And-A-Halfs. Buying them up to close of business Friday 31st, cum the dividend. Selling them on Monday morning, ex the dividend.'

'It doesn't mean anything to me.'

'Frowned on in the City. This guy was so frowned on, he picked up two million quid in six months.'

'Two million?' Hiller stared at him.

Salto nodded. 'And then, about two years after that, I was working for this guy in the East End. We were racing round the betting shops after a jeweller's shop got done. Thirty-four betting shops we made in one afternoon, and got our names down on the books as winners. Fifty-seven grand in quids, all laundered and legal.' He moved closer. 'Now you tell me the difference between those two guys. The guy in the City and the guy in the East End.'

'I don't know.'

'£1,943,000,' Salto said.

Hiller turned away. He felt tired.

But Salto moved round in front of him. 'Don't get the idea I'm a Socialist or anything.' He pointed down at the floor. 'There are a couple of rooms below here, they come with the flat. And when I moved in, there was an old couple living down there. Unfurnished. I couldn't get them out . . . Until I got these Spades to call round with a barrowload of bricks. I needed those two rooms, you see. I needed somewhere to keep my wine.'

Hiller got up. He'd had enough of Salto.

'Where d'you think you're going?'

'To get some sleep. I've been working five hours.'

'You sleep here, where I can see you. Away from the Scotch bottle.'

Salto stood between him and the door. Suddenly he was smiling again.

And Hiller understood. Why Salto had opened a gap in himself, why he'd unloaded his anger. Because he couldn't afford to be angry with Gort. He needed Gort too much.

And just for a moment Salto seemed smaller, a setter-up of deals, crouching in a dirty corner round a phone.

Hiller slept for no more than four hours, then he worked on. Tiredness didn't matter any more. He was a machine, doing a machine's work, moving between the Edit and the code book. By nine in the morning he was almost halfway through. And it was easier now, a lot of the information was repeating.

At ten past nine Gort came in. Salto watched him uneasily. Then he went over to the pile of papers Hiller had de-coded.

'I reckon there's enough here now, isn't there, Gorty? I mean, to start looking round for a Team?'

'I reckon so.' Gort was offhand.

'Who's the first one to go for, then?'

'It has to be the Bellman,' Gort said. 'He's the one who's going to get you in past the Alarm System.'

'All righty, I'll try Coppens.' Salto went over to the phone. 'I ring his agent, don't I? Not the man himself?'

'Always the agent, never direct,' Gort said. 'He takes

care of all the bookings.'

'And I should aim high? To allow for his fifteen per cent?

Gort nodded. 'One more thing. If he's interested, say you'll meet him up West. He won't come down here.'

Salto picked up the phone and dialled a number. 'Could I speak to Mr Samson, please? The name's Salto . . . Salto.'

He waited a moment. And when he spoke again, his voice was careful: 'Mr Samson? You remember we talked about your man? . . . . I think he'll be very interested, Mr Samson. He won't have seen anything like this before . . . No, I don't do business that way. We talk first, and then your man can take a look at what I've got. . . . His standard rate for the job's two per cent of the gross? The gross? Did I hear that right?' He turned to Gort.

Gort shook his head.

'Or in cash, his rate is eighty grand sterling, Mr Samson? Swiss Bank? Of course. . . . Well, I think we've got something to talk about there. . . . And there's the insurance, to cover his equipment, and his wife and kids while he's away? Another seven grand sterling?' Salto cupped his hand over the phone.

'He is the best.' Gort shrugged.

'All right, Mr Samson. It's still a bit heavy. But we can put in the fine print when we meet . . . Oh, and what about dates? When will your man be free? . . . I see. Thank you very much, Mr Samson. I'll get back to you. Goodbye.'

Salto put down the phone. 'We're in business,' he said. 'The Bellman's interested.'

12

Hiller didn't remember finishing, or getting into bed.

He only remembered the moment's panic when he woke. Because he couldn't move, his face was stuck to the pillow, and it hurt as he tore it free. Then he saw the dried blood, and the marks of Gort's beating. He sat up slowly and looked around. On the chair was a tin of Elastoplast and a roll of cotton wool.

He didn't believe the day as he patched up his face and dressed. It was bright, with streaks of cold winter sunlight coming through the window. When he went out, the passage was swept, its walls white and clean. And in the kitchen there was bright coloured paper on the shelves. This end of the flat was an island suddenly, cut off from Salto's shadows and decay.

Anna sat at the kitchen table, writing out a list. As he got nearer, her ballpoint stopped.

Hiller hesitated. For the first time he was close to her, and everything about her seemed foreign to him. Even without make-up, he could see the care that had once gone into her face. The curved eyebrows, the hard grease-pored skin of the actress. And her hair, though matted and lifeless, had once been expensively shaped. He cleared his throat uneasily.

'I just wanted to thank you,' he said.

'Oh? What for?'

'The sticking-plaster and things.'

She didn't look up. She made it plain he could thank her for the plaster, but nothing else. 'You were a mess,' she said. 'I didn't want you frightening the children.'

Hiller turned then. The boy was lying in Mo's shadow that came across the room. She was sitting with her dolls on the window-sill, the sunlight making flames of her hair.

'It's my turn now, isn't it?' she said to the boy.

He nodded.

'All right.' She looked round the room. 'I spy, with my little eye, something beginning with . . . A.'

'Chair,' the boy said.

'No.'

'Table.'

58

'No.'

'Fridge.'

'No.'

'Give up.'

She looked at Hiller. 'You try. Beginning with A.'

'Let's see.' He turned towards the sink. 'Apron?'

'No.'

'Apple?'

'No, *A*. Beginning with *A*.'

'Give up.'

'Radio,' Mo said.

'You do make them very difficult.' Hiller smiled at her.

Then he went over to the boy. 'How are you getting along?'

But there was no greeting. The boy was tense as he looked up, a red patch where his hand had been pressed against his cheek.

'Where's my pocket money?' he asked quietly.

'Oh, dear.' Hiller sat down beside him.

'You must owe me quids by now.'

'Yes.' Hiller was uneasy. In his pocket he counted the eight pound notes and the few coins that were left. 'I wanted to talk to you about that,' he said. 'We could have got it wrong. We could have upped the price too much.'

'You were the one who upped the price.' The boy was angry. 'You were the one who made it ten pounds a day if I didn't run off.'

'I know, but . . .' Hiller was glad their heads were close together, glad that neither Mo nor her mother could hear.

'And you were the one who let me start saving up for that big cabin cruiser. Radio-controlled. Left and right rudder, forward and reverse engines, and the searchlight.'

'Maybe we were aiming too high,' Hiller said.

'Yeh.' The boy turned away. 'When you want me to *do* things I get pocket money. That's the way it is, isn't it?'

'You're right.' Hiller sighed.

He looked round at the sunlight in the kitchen, at Mo leaning against the window pane, drawing matchstick men in her breath. And he felt he had to do something for the boy.

'Look,' he said suddenly. 'How'd it be if I made you a toy? Like those other toys I made you?'

The boy turned back. His voice was loud and excited. 'Like the snake?' he asked. 'The snake that lit up with coloured lights when you shouted at it?'

'Something like that.' Hiller nodded.

Then he looked round. Anna was staring at him strangely.

It took him the rest of the day to make the toy. He had to get the materials for it first, and he didn't even know if Salto would allow him out. But Salto, busy on the phone in the front room, just looked up and nodded. And Hiller left the flat. He walked through the streets until he came to a toy-shop. He bought a Meccano chassis, gears, and wheels. And in a cut-price radio store he found a motor and a photo-electric cell.

In the afternoon he worked in his bedroom. And he enjoyed using a soldering iron again, puffing on his pipe, and making trips to the Scotch bottle in the wardrobe whenever the boy was out. By the time he'd finished it was evening, and he held in his hands a small wheeled vehicle some nine inches long. It had a humped back, and a tubular steel head that ended in a glass eye.

'What is it?' the boy asked.

'A tortoise,' Hiller told him.

He switched it on, and put it down on the floor. The creature whirred, turning its head as if searching for something in the near-darkness. Hiller had a candle ready on a saucer. He lit it, and put it down by a chair. The tortoise looked round, hesitated, and then saw the flame. It went towards it, fussing over the floor in a series of curves, stopping when it lost sight of the candle, and turning its head before moving on again.

Hiller put down more candles, and they confused it.

The tortoise darted around in the centre of the floor, unable to make up its mind.

'That's good.' The boy grinned.

Hiller was lighting another candle by the door, when he heard Anna's voice coming from the kitchen. She was reading a bedtime story to Mo, about Michael Ha'penny and the Nuisance People.

And Hiller straightened. Suddenly he realised he was standing in a dark room where a small machine was trapped midway between two candles. A machine made of metal, and insanely it was angry, clicking its head round from light to light. Then it shook itself free. It moved off, and stopped only when it was right up against a candle. The boy reached out. He tipped the candle over so that the flame was licking the glass eye.

Hiller tried to snatch it away.

'Leave it,' the boy said. 'I like it like that.'

His eyes were bright. The tortoise was swinging its head from side to side in the flame, whining with pleasure.

And from down the hall came Anna's story. The Nuisance People lived in a brown sugar jar. They came out every morning at breakfast time.

It was hopeless.

13

Hiller watched the tortoise move on to another candle and put its head in the flame.

And he thought about the time when he'd courted the boy's mother.

The strange time.

He'd been thirty-eight, she thirty-six, and the boy five

years old.

He thought of the strange conversations he'd had with her on the phone.

'Will I see you tomorrow?' he'd asked.

'Yes. I bought a coat at John Lewis',' she'd replied. She was with the boy's father, in the same room, and she couldn't talk.

'Tomorrow at nine? The usual place?'

'Yes. It's got blue buttons down the front. *Yes*.'

If you'd asked him, Hiller wouldn't say he'd had an unhappy life. No more or less unhappy than anyone else's. It was just that there'd been no printed invitations, no weddings or changes-of-address, no white gateposts and no-one to tell.

There hadn't been the time. There'd only been time for escaping from the terraced house in Reading. The years of night-school. Then the years of travelling Europe as an installation-engineer. Which was the job no-one wanted, because it meant six months in a strange town, then six months in another.

And when he'd returned to England at the age of twenty-eight, he suddenly found he was five years out of step. He was looking for a wife, and they were having children. And later, when he was desperate, they were desperate too. But in another way.

He'd met the boy's mother at a shadowy suburban party where husbands and wives were bored and clutching at strangers. But she hadn't been like the others, she was sitting alone. Later he found out she was warm, attractive, and honest, the most honest woman he'd ever met. She was also unhappy, her life governed by a husband who came and went. Between them they'd thrown out every rule of married life – except one. She felt bad about the boy, and she wasn't going to leave home.

But Hiller had persuaded her. He told her he wanted her and the boy, both. And he'd married her finally. He was earning good money too, by this time, and he went after those white gateposts. He rented a house with a garden, he made a sandpit and a swing. And for the first four years he thought they had a chance.

Because he didn't mind about the occasional men, he'd never blamed her for that. And he knew that his drinking – which was no more than the drinking of any other installation-engineer – didn't help him in bed. So every now and then they'd gone their separate ways in the evenings. She, out once the boy was asleep. And he to the huge gramophone and the records he'd always promised himself.

Until the night when he'd walked out of a room filled with Wagner and gone upstairs. The boy was awake. He'd been awake every night his mother was out, waiting for her to return. And Hiller had begun the stories then. With his voice loud with whisky, with Wagner booming out from down below, he'd turned the boy's mother into a Princess.

And that's what she'd never been able to forgive him for – the happy endings. The way he'd shaved away his hangovers in the morning and never asked her about the night before. The way he'd built strange mechanical toys for the boy. The way the garden was now crowded with a fort and a pirate's cave as well as the sandpit and swing. And the way the stories had grown to include a whole army of characters.

'But it's not true,' she'd shouted. 'None of it's true.'

Hiller knew it. The boy knew it. But the Princess, Sooty Ann Gorge, Mousey Tongue, and Alcide Slow Drag Pavageau, were all that they had together.

'Tell us a story.'

'What?' Hiller looked up. The boy was sitting facing him. And he was bored. The tortoise had run down, the candles were guttering around the room.

'Tell us a story.'

'Not just at the moment. I don't feel like it.'

'Why not?'

'I don't know. Later. Maybe I'll do it later.' He got up

and blew the candles out, one by one. It was dark then, there was just the light coming down the hallway from the kitchen.

'Go on.'

'I told you, I don't feel like it.' Hiller looked at his watch. 'Anyway it's too early. We don't usually have our stories till later on.'

'It's not too early. Mo's having hers next door.'

And Hiller heard it then, Anna still reading the same story in the kitchen.

'Why don't you go in there and listen with her?' he asked.

'That crap?' the boy sneered. 'That Michael Ha'penny crap?'

Hiller didn't answer.

'Go on. Tell us our story. Our one. The Continuing Saga Of Sod's Law.'

'Not right now.'

'Tell us about the Princess.'

'Later.'

'The Princess. Go on.'

There was silence in the room. Just Anna's voice coming through the door. A quiet family voice, with its back to the world. And Hiller couldn't help it:

'She went away with a gentleman,' he said softly, too softly for the boy to hear.

'What?'

'Nothing.'

But the boy had ears like a cat. 'She went away?'

He stood there, caught by the strip of light from the doorway. His mouth was open, his eyes racing to catch up. 'Went *away*?'

And Hiller was frightened. Because that broke all the rules. The Princess could go to garden parties in a giraffe-skin coat. She could drink wine that tasted like a frosty morning. But she couldn't go away. Not as she had done in real life.

'I didn't say that,' he lied.

'Yes, you did.'

'All right, I did. But it wasn't important. Just a tiny part of the story.'

'Tell me then.'

'Get into bed first.'

The boy did so, without taking off his clothes. And Hiller went to the wardrobe to find the Scotch bottle. There were only four mouthfuls left. He swallowed them quickly.

'There was something else you said. About a gentleman.'

'Oh, that?' The sudden rush of whisky put words in his mouth: 'Gentlemen can do any bloody thing. Gentlemen lift the sea.'

'Sea? What d'you mean? Is that part of the story too?'

'Yes.' Hiller was desperate. 'Only I got the end bit first. I got it all mixed up.'

'Start at the beginning then. With the Princess going away.'

'Well, the Princess . . .' He looked round at the shadows, searching for a way out. '. . . *Why* she went away was she wasn't just a Princess, she was a Secret Agent too.'

There was a long pause. Then the boy breathed out. 'I knew it,' he said.

Hiller sat down by the bed, sweating.

'And what did she do? As a Secret Agent?'

'She was on our side, of course,' Hiller said. 'And she was against Them.'

'Them? These Gentlemen you were on about?'

'That's it. A question of World Domination. The Highest Priority.'

'Lifting the sea?'

'Christ.' Hiller turned away. 'Lifting the sea, yes . . . Yes, they were going to flood London, you see. Pull the plug out of the Central Line, between Theydon Bois and Ongar.'

'What's an Ongar?'

'Nobody's sure. Nobody who's been there has ever

come back.'

'I see.' The boy didn't see at all, but his voice was easier now. 'And how was the Princess mixed up in it all?'

'She was the one who found the vital clue.'

'The what?'

'There has to be a vital clue in these things,' Hiller said. 'In this case it was the fingerprints on Leroy's trouser-press.'

'I don't get it.'

'Well, Leroy, he was Number One World Dominator. It's true he started out small, just dominating dogs and old ladies. But then he got onto dominating bigger things, Staines Reservoir and the Egham By-Pass. And then finally, it had to be the works, London and the whole world.'

'And you mean, the Princess was against him?'

'That's right.'

'And that's why she had to leave?'

Hiller nodded. 'She got a signal from Headquarters to move out.'

'What was the signal?'

'A scent-spray like a lighter, with coloured stars on it.' Hiller's voice shook. He could see it then, just as it was when she'd got it from her handbag.

'And where did she go to?' the boy asked.

'To a house.'

'What house?'

He didn't answer.

'What house was it?'

And all at once the months of anger rose up in Hiller. 'A house shaped like a bloody juke-box,' he said savagely. 'Where a hundred guitars full of Hobo juice were playing Ape-Real Love . . .'

He stopped then. Because the boy understood. He was sitting very still, hunched up on the bed in a tight ball, his arms locked across his knees. Hiller had never seen him like that before.

'Maybe it wasn't like that,' he said quickly. 'Maybe I

got it wrong.'

The boy turned away.

'Don't you want me to go on?'

'No.'

'I mean, we're coming to the good part. Where we meet up with the Princess again.'

'I don't want to hear any more,' the boy said.

'Not tomorrow, either?'

'No.'

14

'Hiller baby. Hiller baby.'

Salto was there suddenly, standing against the white passage wall, invading this end of the flat with his tiredness and his stale cigar smoke.

'What is it?' Hiller asked.

'I want to talk to you.'

'Not here.' He pointed round at the boy.

'All righty.' Salto went towards the light from the kitchen. Hiller got up and followed him in there.

Then they both stopped. Anna was sitting at the table, eating her supper.

'Baby,' Salto smiled at her, 'would you mind leaving us a moment? So we can have a little heart to heart?'

She left her meal unfinished and walked past them to the door.

Hiller sat down.

Salto watched him a moment. 'I'm after some advice, dear Heart.'

'Advice?' Hiller didn't understand.

'Technical stuff,' Salto said. 'I mean, you cracked that Print-Out, didn't you? You must have understood the technical stuff in there.'

'I suppose so.'

'What d'you mean, you suppose so? Did you understand it or didn't you?'

'I'm an engineer.' Hiller nodded.

'All right then,' Salto said. 'Well, the thing is, this Bellman I've hired. He . . .'

'. . . Bellman?'

Salto leaned over him suddenly. 'Have you been drinking?'

'No. I had a couple, that's all. Some time ago.'

'What's the matter then?'

'Nothing.'

Salto looked at him carefully. 'Tell you what,' he said. 'I'm in to you for two hundred quid, aren't I? So I'll up it another fifty for some advice. Five minutes work. How's that?'

Fifty quid for five minutes advice. Hiller didn't need to think about it very long. 'What d'you want to know?' he asked.

Salto sat on the edge of the table and lit a cigar. 'We'll start at the beginning,' he said. 'A Bellman is a man who specialises in burglar alarms. Right?'

'If you say so.'

'And this one I've hired, he's the best in the business. He's looked through that stuff you did for me, and he says it's very good, the best he's seen. . . . Except for one thing. He says if he's to get us in past the alarm-system, there's something else he needs to know. A call-sign.'

'I see.' Hiller thought for a moment. 'He could be right, I suppose.'

'Why's that?'

'Well, how much d'you know about bank alarms?'

'Not a lot.'

Hiller scrubbed a hand tiredly across his forehead. 'Going by what I saw, I'd say they were very complicated things. It's not just bells that go off when you break a window. It's scanners that can cover every inch of a room.

It's strong-room doors that release a partial vacuum when you try to open them. There's no way at all you can get round those. No way you can even get near them.'

'So?'

'So, I'd say your friend was trying to get at the wires leading to those alarms, bridge them in some way.'

'He did talk about bridging. What's it mean?'

'You tap the wire before the alarm,' Hiller said. 'You tap it after the alarm. And you connect up. That way you by-pass the whole thing, and it can't go off.'

'Why doesn't he just do that then?'

'It's not that simple. It isn't just a wire carrying an electric current. It's a wire carrying a signal. That's the thing.'

'You've lost me,' Salto said.

Hiller sighed. 'There's a bank. And there's a signal coming into it along a wire. This signal, it's like a question. It goes to each of the alarms in turn and asks if they're all right. Once it gets the answers, it leaves the bank again, and goes along a wire to a monitor station miles away. . . . Now, if everything's all right, if the answers from all of the alarms are Yes, then that's it. No red lights flashing on the monitor desk. Everything normal.'

'All right. And how often does this question-and-answer bit happen?'

'About 200 times a second.'

Salto whistled.

'It's not the speed that's the trouble,' Hiller said. 'If your man's good, he can get into the wire and listen to the signal. But the thing is, he's got to identify it. Exactly the right questions coming in, and the right questions-and-answers coming out. That's the only way he can take the alarms out of circuit. And how's he going to do that?'

'How d'you mean?'

'The bank isn't the only building on this wire-system. There are other banks, post offices, jewellers, gunsmiths maybe. I'm guessing now, but I'd say there could be fifty other places.'

'Fifty?'

'In a fair-sized town. So that's fifty signals, each with a code, say, of five hundred digits. And they can come in any order along the wire, the circuits are changing all the time. So how the hell's your man going to tell which one's which?'

There was a pause. Then Salto got there. 'Each building's got its own call-sign,' he said.

Hiller nodded.

'And you mean, it's that important?'

'Of course it is. If your man doesn't know the bank's call-sign, he's going to have red lights flashing all over the place.'

'I see.' Salto looked down at the end of his cigar. 'It wasn't included in the Print-Out then? This call-sign?'

'Why should it be? It's got nothing to do with the bank itself. It's worked out by the man on the monitor desk, away in the police station or wherever.'

'No, it's not the police any more,' Salto said. 'They've passed all that sort of stuff over to the Noddy Men.'

'The who?'

'The security firms. It seems it's got too complicated for the Law to handle. There've been too many false alarms.'

And Hiller could believe it. He remembered one of the alarm-systems he'd copied out of the Print-Out. An ultrasonic alarm called a VSU. There was nothing simple about that.

'If it was the Law, Christ, it'd be easy,' Salto said angrily. 'You want to find out something like this call-sign, and you can always find a bent copper. But you try finding a bent Noddy Man. The ones in the know, they get paid too much, and they're watched over like bloody schoolkids.'

He turned away and stubbed his cigar out viciously. 'So what you're trying to tell me is we're all in schtuck without this call-sign? There's no other way?'

And Hiller shouldn't have answered. It was when he saw the cigar-stub in Anna's half-eaten supper. 'For God's sake,' he said, 'any machine can go wrong.'

'What d'you mean?'

'Nothing.'

'You started to say something.' Salto grabbed his arm.

'It's just that . . .'

'Just that what?'

'Well, all my life I've repaired machines,' Hiller said. 'Machines ten times as complicated as those in the bank. And they were always going wrong.'

'I don't get you.'

'You said yourself there'd been a lot of false alarms. That means the systems were going wrong somewhere, doesn't it?'

'So?'

'So, all you have to do is to arrange a false alarm. Find some way of putting the system on the blink.'

Salto sat quite still. 'You got any ideas, dear Heart?'

'No.'

'You're quite sure about that?'

'Yes.'

But he was lying. And Salto knew it. Because at the back of Hiller's mind was the alarm called a VSU. And against that, a much smaller machine. The toy he'd built for the boy this afternoon. The tortoise.

Salto got up, no longer menacing him. 'I'd be willing to pay money for the right idea,' he said quietly. 'You should remember that.'

'I can't help you,' Hiller said.

'I'll ask you again tomorrow, dear Heart.' He paused a moment in the doorway. 'A bit drab, your life here with us, wouldn't you say? A bit on the drab side?'

Hiller didn't answer.

15

And the next morning was drab. The sunlight had gone, rain beat steadily against the kitchen window, and Mo stared out at it unhappily. She kept singing the same two words, over and over again:

'Ruby too, Ruby too, Ruby too.'

'Stop it,' her mother said. 'You're bothering people.'

'I aren't.' She turned away. 'Ruby too, Ruby too, Ruby too . . .' She went on until she ran out of breath.

'What is it?' Hiller asked her. 'A song?'

'About this man, Ken John Peel.' She nodded.

'You mean . . . D'you ken John Peel?'

'No, it's . . . Yes, I ken John Peel and Ruby too, Ranter and Ringwood, Bellman and True.'

'Oh, the second verse,' Hiller said. 'I see.'

'Ruby too, Ruby too, Ruby . . .'

'. . . That's enough,' her mother cut her short. 'Why don't you go and find something to do?'

'What is there?' Mo looked round at the grey room.

'What about your Elastics? You were playing that yesterday.'

'I can't play it on my own.'

'No.'

And they both turned to where the boy was sitting over by the door, alone.

'He won't play with me,' Mo said, 'not all day.'

There was a moment's silence. Hiller wanted to end it. 'I'll play with you,' he said.

'Elastics?' Mo was eager.

'If you like.'

She went to the table and came back with a loop of knicker elastic, a yard long. She trapped one end of it around the back legs of a chair, and showed Hiller how to stand inside the other end so that his ankles held the loop taut, just off the ground.

'What Elastics d'you want to see?' she asked.

'I don't know. What ones are there?'

'There's Ankles, and there's Knees. French Knees or German Knees.'

'Let's see French Knees,' Hiller said.

She looked at the loop of elastic. 'It has to be higher for Knees.'

'Oh.' He looked down too. 'Are you sure you'll be able to jump it?'

'Ye-es.' She wasn't sure at all.

Hiller bent and worked the elastic up his legs a little. A very little, no more than an inch. 'There. That's Knees,' he said.

Mo nodded at him gratefully.

She stood outside the loop, very close to it. She gathered herself, legs together, and jumped. A tiny jump that didn't clear it.

'Nearly,' Hiller said.

Then he looked round. And for the first time he saw Anna smile. It wasn't for him, he knew, and the lines of her face hadn't softened much. But beauty had a hard face nowadays, he told himself, it was the fashion.

Mo jumped on.

She gasped for breath as her legs darted in and out of the elastic, twisting it into a strange cat's cradle. Finally she tired and looked round at her mother. 'Did you see?'

'Yes,' Anna said. But she hadn't, she'd been watching the boy. 'Is he all right?' she asked.

'Yes, I think so.'

'Are you sure?' She turned her back on the children and lowered her voice. 'I mean, is it anything we've done?'

'No,' Hiller went over to her. 'Sometimes he gets like that. Don't worry about it.'

'But he doesn't say much, does he?'

'He's never said very much. There was a time . . .' He tailed away.

'Was a time what?'

'It doesn't matter. Just something that used to make me laugh.'

'Tell me.'

'Well, there was a time when he only said five words . . . Me, more, mine, stuck, and bugger.'

It was a moment before he could look at her. But when he did, he saw she was smiling again. Only this time her mouth was warm and full, and all for him.

'It's true,' he said. 'I know it's funny, but it's true.'

And for the first time he felt close to her.

Then suddenly she was looking past him. He heard the scream. He swung round.

Mo was on the floor. The boy was on top of her, going at her savagely with his fists.

Anna was a full second in front of Hiller. And he didn't recognise her any more. She grabbed the boy by his hair and smacked him hard with the back of her hand, again and again. Hiller had to tear him free.

'Get him out of here,' she said.

In the bedroom the boy sat as far away from Hiller as he could, pressed up against the wall.

'What did you bloody do that for?' Hiller asked.

'Because I bloody felt like it bloody.'

And he was right. There wasn't any point in talking like that. 'Tell me what the matter is.' Hiller lowered his voice.

The boy shook his head.

'Are you hurt?'

He was hurt. There were bruises under his eyes. But it wasn't that.

It was the way he was sitting on the bed, hunched up in a tight ball.

'Is it last night?' Hiller asked.

The boy didn't answer.

'I mean, the story last night?'

He still didn't answer.

'Look,' Hiller said, 'when I told you about the Princess . . .' He didn't finish. He could hear how useless the word was in the cold light of day.

The boy could hear it too.

'What I meant about the Princess,' Hiller tried again, 'was I didn't get to the end of it. Because we do meet up with her again. We really do.'

The boy didn't believe him. He was crying. But his eyes were strangely hard behind his tears, disowning them.

'It's true,' Hiller said. 'We meet up with her in this country.' He looked at the rain beating against the window. 'A country where it's always sunny.'

'Crap.'

'I mean it. The skies are always blue in this country. And . . . And there are toffee apple trees.'

'Crap.'

It wasn't any good, Hiller knew that. He couldn't do it without the Scotch bottle or the cover of darkness.

He got up and went to the window. He stared at the dark clouds, the buildings streaked with rain. And the greyness of it got through to him.

He remembered when he'd worked as an engineer. All the cities he'd stayed in alone, a long time ago.

'There isn't a country, is there?' the boy asked.

'Yes, there is,' Hiller said.

'You're only saying that.'

But he wasn't. Because suddenly he remembered the one city where spring had followed winter, and where he'd found just the one warm corner. 'There's a country all right,' he said. 'I saw a bit of it once.'

'What d'you mean, a bit of it?'

'Well, it isn't all in one place.' Hiller still looked out of the window. 'There are bits of it everywhere, all over the world. You have to come across them by accident.'

'You mean, with all that blue sky crap? That toffee-apple crap you were on about?'

'No, not that. I got that bit wrong.' Hiller was speaking softly. 'It's a country where all the best things are less rather than more. Where people don't take more than there is to take.'

'What are you on about?'

He didn't answer. He turned back towards the boy.

'I mean, what's so special about this country of yours?'

'It isn't anything you'd understand.'

'What's so bloody special? Go on, you started it. Tell me.'

Hiller stared at the pale thin face, at the tears that couldn't seem to touch it. And he knew he had to go on.

'There's a city called Athens. I used to work there. And . . .' He shrugged. It wasn't going to work.

'And what?'

'Well, if you want to know, I only had a couple of friends there. They were in the same line of business, they used to go round the clubs in the evenings, and I didn't like that very much. So I used to get on a trolley bus and go out to this place.'

'What place?'

'It wasn't much. No more than a café, really. But there was dancing.'

'Dancing?'

'Only men dancing, no girls,' Hiller said quickly. 'You see, you made a long queue, if you were men, all holding hands.'

'Bloody holding. . . ?'

'. . . D'you want to hear it or don't you?' Hiller pressed his knuckles against his forehead. 'All right, you made this long queue and you danced. But the thing was, if you wanted to dance the fiddly bits, you had to go up to the head of the queue. And to do that you had to pay, push some money through the hole of the guitar-player's guitar.' He went towards the boy, willing him to understand. 'And you see, most of the men there were workmen, and they only pushed a couple of pence in the guitar. But there were just a couple of men in smart city suits. And they had to pay more, just to show they were smart. And once I saw a man pay £5, and dance £5. He really did, and everyone knew it.'

The boy sat quite still.

Hiller waited, bending over him.

'Is that *all*?' the boy shouted suddenly. 'Is that bloody *all*?'

Hiller stepped back.

'Because it's *nothing*.' The boy stood up, tiny with his anger. 'Like every other thing you told me about. Like the pocket money I was going to get. Like that big boat, radio-controlled. Like all the stories about the Princess and the rest. *Nothing*. *None* of them was true.'

Hiller took another step back, clumsily, knocking over a chair. There was only one precise thing about him at that moment, and that was the way his hands moved, setting the chair to rights. The rest of him was white and flabby, the panic spilling out of him.

Because there was that look on the boy's face.

The same look.

'It's not true,' his mother had shouted. 'None of it's true.'

He faced the boy now. Neither of them moved. The silence stretched right through the flat.

Then, for some reason, in Hiller's mind came the words of a song. The song Mo had been singing. Ruby too, Ruby too.

And slowly he straightened up. 'Oh, yes, it's true all right,' he said.

'What d'you mean?'

'Bellman and True.'

The boy didn't understand. .

'And what that means is,' Hiller stood over him, 'you're going to get all that pocket money I promised you. And you're going to get that big radio-controlled boat. And what's more, when we leave here, you and I, we're going to have two plane tickets. We're going to get on an airliner and fly up in the sky.'

'A real airliner?'

'That's right. We're going to go over the sea to this country I was talking about. We're going to look for the right part of it, and then we're going to try and find the Princess. I promise you that.'

He left the boy then and went to the front room.

Salto and Gort were sitting together in the shadows. They had their backs to the bay window and the greyness outside.

Hiller stood between them. 'All right, I'll do it,' he said.

'Do what?' Salto looked up.

'Tell you how to get into the bank.'

Nobody moved. There was just the sound of the rain.

Then Salto got to his feet. 'You do surprise me, Hearty. You really do surprise me.'

'I didn't finish,' Hiller said. 'I'll want money, a lot of money. And I'll want to get out of the country afterwards, with the boy.'

'All right.' Salto moved round so he had Hiller's face in the light. 'Tell you what I'll do. If your idea's any good, I'll slip you a few quid. How's that?'

Hiller nerved himself. '£20,000,' he said. 'A quarter of what you were going to pay Coppens.'

Gort stopped chewing suddenly. 'Coppens? For Christ's sake, he was in here, wasn't he? When you were doing the phoning?'

Hiller nodded. 'A quarter of £80,000. The union rate.'

Salto laughed. But it wasn't funny. 'You don't know what you're talking about. Coppens is the top boy. He gets the top money.'

'Take it or leave it,' Hiller said.

Salto looked at him closely. 'Something's got into you, dear Heart, hasn't it?'

'That's right.'

'But ten grand? Just for information? Telling us how to get in?'

'No, I'll do more than that. Much more. I'll throw in the

78

device as well.'

'What device?'

'The device that sets the bank's alarms on the blink.'
Hiller thought for a moment. 'I can make it up from a
couple of children's toys. One's a thing called a tortoise.
And the other's a toy cabin cruiser, radio controlled.'

16

Back in the kitchen Hiller sank onto a chair, exhausted,
needing a drink. Anna was alone in the room. She came
over.

'I'm sorry I hit your kid,' she said. 'I don't approve of
hitting other peoples' kids.'

'Nor do I,' Hiller told her. 'That's why I don't.'

'What d'you mean?'

And perhaps it was the exhaustion that made it easy to
talk. 'He's not my kid,' he said. 'He's my stepson. His
mother went off.'

'Oh.' There was no surprise in her voice. It was as if she
was used to hearing things like that.

'Anyway he's been hit before. He's used to it,' Hiller
went on. 'She used to slap him around, you see. Not
through anger, through fear. What he was, I mean. She
never wanted him in the first place.' He stared at his
hands. 'And all the time he idolised her. I never could
understand that.'

'No. Well, she's his mother.' Anna turned her back. 'It's
the same with Mo in a way. She only sees what she wants
to. Not what there is.'

She walked away from him slowly, over to the window.
'This place we were renting before,' she said then, 'it was
too pricey. And sometimes I had to go back to the old way,

take on a client, just to pay the rent.'

Hiller was embarrassed, but she went on.

'Mo, she used to see me suddenly in the clothes, the hair-do, the eyelashes out to here.' She shrugged. 'And Mo, she still reckons everybody goes off on honeymoon in a balloon, like in the Babar books.'

She was smiling as she came back towards him. 'Anyway, it's different now. They're paying me to look after your kid. I've got a little put by. Maybe it'll be enough to get away somewhere and start again. Somewhere quiet.'

'Is that what you want?'

She nodded. 'And what about you?'

'Well, it'll be a week or two yet,' Hiller said uneasily. 'I mean, before I'm finished here.'

'But I thought you were finished. I thought you'd given them that computer thing you were working on.'

Hiller didn't answer. He couldn't meet her eyes.

'You're not getting in deep with them, are you?' She bent over him suddenly.

'Why? Why d'you ask?'

'Because they're not your style, that's why. Any silly sod can see that.' The swearword twisted her mouth. He was strangely affected by it, by her concern.

17

In the late afternoon Salto came for him. 'Get your coat on,' he said. 'We're going out.'

'Out? Out where?'

'Up West,' Salto said.

And Hiller was nervous as they went out to the waiting taxi. It moved slowly at first through the rush-hour traffic, but then they took the Ring Road that ran above the roof-tops. The tarmac was strangely white up there, washed by the rain. And high overhead was a huge gunmetal cloud, a dark lid keeping the city on the boil.

They came down into a maze of shadowy streets. Salto paid off the taxi on the edge of a market, and they walked along pavements that were mushy with torn cardboard boxes. Around them the hawkers' voices were angry, trying to make up for lost time after the rain.

There was a young man standing in a wet doorway, shouting at a crowd. 'There's your Dior. There's your Fabergé.' He held up two bottles of scent. 'As advertised by Selfridges at ten pound . . . I don't want to hear about ten pound. I don't want to hear about four pound . . . Stolen property. If you never bought stolen property before, now's your chance.'

Beyond him in a narrow alley was a pub. It was quiet inside, men who were strangers to each other drank quickly before going home. And on the bar was a small lit sign, YOUR HOSTS: JIMBO ~~AND MARGIE~~. DON'T BE VAGUE, ASK FOR HAIG. Hiller didn't have time to ask for anything. Because a man came up, a man with wet grey hair he mopped with a handkerchief. Mr Samson.

'They're waiting for you upstairs,' he said.

The room upstairs was long and dark, hardboard panels blocked out most of the window. There was a band-stand hung with silver paper, tables and chairs around the walls. And sitting at one of them, in shadow, was a group of men.

Mr Samson left Hiller by the window and took Salto on towards the men. They sat down, Salto being careful, keeping just outside the circle as he talked. No-one looked round at Hiller.

And he was more than nervous now. Because the names he'd heard – the pantomime names – Bellman, Peterman, Guv'nor, Stoppo, and Donkey – didn't seem to fit any more. These were middle-aged men, rich, in expensive suits. But what was wrong was that they had none of the ease that should have gone with the suits. They were tense, they sat in empty dance-halls at lino-topped tables, and they talked behind their hands.

It was easy to see which one was the Donkey. He was huge as he stood up, with a white slab face. He leaned over the man next to him and showed him an empty cigarette packet. 'Lend us some fag-money,' he said. 'I come out with the wrong suit.'

The man shook his head. 'It's always the same with you.'

The Donkey moved on. He tried the other men round the table, but had no luck. Then he went out. Nobody missed him. Nobody looked round at Hiller. The talk went on.

Hiller turned away to the window. On the far side of the alley was a strip club. There were coloured bulbs round a doorway, and a young Greek with a microphone wheedling at the passers-by. They didn't stop, they looked round at the pictures a moment, but kept on walking.

Then there was shouting, a swirl in the crowd as they backed away from the club doorway. And suddenly an elderly man in a Homburg hat was dumped on the pavement. Behind him the Greek disappeared, the door closed, the coloured lights went out. The man sat there, his fawn coat strangely clean on the pavement, one shin showing white above his sock. Then a trickle of blood came from his mouth. People saw it as they passed, but none of them stopped. Until a young couple bent over him and a crowd gathered. The man was helped to his feet, a broken denture sticking out of his mouth like a claw as he said 'No, no . . .' He staggered away, his briefcase scraping the wall.

Hiller realised someone was standing next to him, one of the men from the table. He was in his forties, broad-shouldered, and taut in a shiny suit. His face was white, potbound, a face of waiting veins. And as he looked down at the alley his eyes were hard with other peoples' weaknesses. They were all he saw, they were his trade. He was the Guv'nor.

82

He turned now and stared down the length of the dark room at the door, waiting for it to open. The Donkey came in. He had a cigarette in his mouth, and he came over, offering a full packet. The Guv'nor grabbed his hand, turned it over, and saw the skinned knuckles. Suddenly his fist went back, high, the whole way. He smashed it into the Donkey, low in the groin.

The Donkey went down. A roll of £5 notes rode up from his front pocket.

'Dirty fugging scruff,' the Guv'nor shouted. 'You pull another stroke like that and I break your fugging back.'

Breathing hard, he turned to Hiller and motioned him towards the table. As they went over, Hiller found it was Salto who was doing the talking.

'But that's the whole thing,' he was saying. 'It doesn't have to be a big London bank, or Birmingham. It can be some place out in the sticks where they've suddenly come into the money. Somewhere they don't know us, where they wouldn't be expecting us in a hundred years . . . Because there are banks like that. We found them in the Print-Out.'

Hiller sat down. There was silence. They were all watching him.

'Get on with it,' the Guv'nor said.

Hiller couldn't. His mouth was dry, he couldn't speak.

'About the alarms,' Mr Samson said.

Hiller looked up. He saw Mr Samson was sitting close to another man, talking for him. Coppens, the Bellman. And Coppens was old. His white hair went back in straight lines on his skull, heavily greased, but without shine. His cheeks were paper thin, his mouth genteel, and as he smoked he flicked ash carefully away from his dark pinstripe suit. There was something of the school-master about him.

Hiller felt the sweat trickling down his sides. He remembered how it always had been at school. The dark figure on the dais calling for someone to own up. And Hiller, innocent, but his cheeks flaming, being singled out.

Suddenly he realised that now he was going to settle the debt.

He got his mind working on the Print-Out, the black columns of data. 'This machinery in the bank,' he began shakily, 'It's very complicated. I don't think you're going to be able to get round it.'

'We know that,' Mr Samson said.

'And you're not going to be able to bridge any of the wires. Not unless you get hold of the call-sign.'

'We know that too.'

Hiller tried to steady his voice. He had to tell them something they didn't know. 'But there's another way of looking at it. I mean, you spend all your time trying not to trigger the alarms off . . . But in theory it'd be much simpler if they *were* all triggered off. All of them. All the time.'

'What's he talking about?' The Guv'nor swung round.

'If every alarm in that bank was set off,' Hiller said, 'then they wouldn't be guarding anything, would they? and all you'd have to do would be to open doors.'

'For Christ's sake, what's he talking about?'

Hiller turned to Coppens. The man's eyes showed nothing, but his cigarette stopped an inch away from his mouth, and stayed there.

'I'm talking about a false alarm,' Hiller told him. 'And it'll have to be intermittent. One that malfunctions every twenty minutes, on the dot, and functions perfectly for the rest of the time.'

'You mean, that can happen?' the Guv'nor asked.

Coppens nodded.

'And what d'you think the security procedure would be then?' Hiller asked. 'In the case of this false alarm?'

'You tell us,' the Guv'nor said.

'All right. From what I saw in the Print-Out, I'd say it'd go like this. . .' Hiller counted off each point on his fingers. '. . . An alarm triggers off in the bank . . . A red light flashes in the monitor-station miles away . . . The man on the monitor desk presses the Alarm button . . . A mobile unit goes along to the bank, and they go in . . . But they find nothing. No doors or windows forced, nobody inside. *And* the alarm's now working perfectly again . . . So, what do they do? They signal back to the monitor-station that it's a malfunction, a false alarm that's come and gone.'

'And what good does that do us?'

'Well, the first thing is they're not suspicious,' Hiller said. 'And the second thing is that the red light's been flashing in the monitor station all this time. And it's still flashing. It's programmed to start as soon as the alarm triggers off, and go on continuously until the fault is checked and identified. An automatic fail-safe device.' He paused. 'So, when the signal comes in from the mobile unit that the false alarm's over, that everything's working perfectly again. Then the man on the monitor desk has to switch over to a second line coming from the bank. This line's clear, of course, and the red light stops flashing . . . Situation normal. And the man on the desk tells the mobile unit they can lock up and leave the bank.'

He was talking to Coppens now, the only man who understood. And Coppens was sitting quite still. Ash fell from his cigarette, but he made no move to brush it off.

'An intermittent false alarm,' Hiller went on. 'Twenty minutes later we arrange another one . . . Again the red light flashes on the desk. Again the mobile unit goes in and reports all clear. And now the man on the desk has to switch over to the third line coming from the bank, so he can clear the flashing light.' He stared at Coppens. 'And there are only four lines, aren't there? The system's only laid in quadruplicate.'

Coppens nodded.

'So we reach a situation after the fourth false alarm,' Hiller said it very slowly, 'when the red light's flashing all the time.' He looked round at the others. 'Any alarm in the building can be tampered with, and it won't show. Nobody's suspicious. The bank's wide open.'

'You mean that?' the Guv'nor asked.

Hiller nodded. 'The machine's broken down. And all

they can do now is rely on men.'

'Men?' The Guv'nor hissed in breath. 'For Christ's sake, they'll send that mobile unit back, won't they? Noddy Men, with crash-hats and weighted pick-axe handles. That's not our style at all.'

'Men are a lot easier to handle than machines,' Hiller said. 'Because if you look at the Print-Out, you'll see that the security men can only get into a limited area of the ground floor, the entrances and the exits. They haven't got the keys to go any further.' He spread his hands. 'The rest of the building's yours.'

He sat back then. There was silence round the table. They were all looking at Coppens.

And Coppens spoke for the first time. Suddenly he was no longer the school-master. Behind the dark pinstripe suit and the silk shirt, his voice was East End. It shouldn't have been a surprise.

'How're you going to do it?' he asked Hiller. 'These false alarms you were on about, one every twenty minutes, how're you going to work them?'

'You'd use a device, wouldn't you?'

'What sort of a device.'

Hiller told him. And Coppens, small and frail behind his cigarette, lit one after another, quickly, trying not to see the harm they were doing him.

His face showed nothing when Hiller had finished. He sat there for a moment, thinking. Then he leaned forward.

'You didn't say about the other thing.'

'What other thing?' Hiller asked.

'The closed circuit TV. The screens they got on the monitor desk, and in the bank.'

'You could take care of that. Break into the cable somewhere.'

'How?'

'You'd have to be careful. It's hooked up to a status-detector system, isn't it? Like every other cable in the bank?' Hiller thought back to the Print-Out. 'In this case it's a co-ax cable screened by a high-frequency pulse.'

'And?'

'You'd use an oscilloscope and a simulator. Well, wouldn't you?'

'You would.' Coppens nodded.

Hiller didn't understand why he'd asked. It was simple. He must have known the answer already.

But he wasn't given a chance to understand. Coppens flapped a hand, and Hiller was led away to the door. It was as sudden as that.

Downstairs in the Saloon he started on the whisky. He was trembling as he leaned against the bar by the small lit sign, YOUR HOSTS: JIMBO ~~AND MARGIE~~. And Jimbo, who'd scratched out her name in anger, was behind the counter. He was a sour man, carrying his weight on the heels of his hands while he watched people sit. He'd brought Hiller three large whiskies by the time Salto arrived.

Salto paid for the fourth and led Hiller away to the shadows. 'It's all right,' he said quietly. 'It's going to work.'

'Oh?'

'He likes it. His actual words were . . . very shrewd, very shrewd indeed.'

'That's good then.'

But it wasn't good. Salto's voice was too quiet. And there was the other thing – the question Coppens had asked upstairs, about the TV cable.

'What's up?' Salto was watching him. 'You're not going to back out now, are you?'

'No.'

'And you'll set it up for us, like you said? Show us how to work it?'

'If you keep to your side of it,' Hiller said.

'Ah yes, the money.' Salto chewed on a nail. 'We said twenty grand, didn't we?'

'We did.'

Hiller waited. He wondered what he'd have to settle for. Ten grand? Six?

'Twenty grand it is then,' Salto said.

Hiller stared at him. He was beginning to think something was wrong.

'Then there's the insurance too.' Salto got an envelope from his pocket. 'Everybody gets that. It comes on top.'

Hiller took the envelope and opened it inside his coat. They were £20 notes, forty of them. More money than he'd ever held in his life.

Salto went to the door and Hiller followed him. It was night outside. Beyond the lights of the alley the street was dark, the market had moved on.

Except for the young man selling bottles of scent. 'Stolen property,' he shouted. 'If you never bought stolen property before, now's your chance.'

18

Something was wrong. Hiller knew it when Salto came for him the next morning.

He took him out of the flat and along the pavement to a parked van. The Guv'nor was waiting there, hunched up against the grey sky and the wind. He opened the rear door and motioned Hiller inside. 'Just you,' he said.

But Hiller hung back. 'What's going on?' he asked Salto.

'Nothing. Nothing to worry about.'

'Yes, but . . .'

'It's all right,' Salto said.

'Get in.' The Guv'nor pushed him inside.

It was a hire-van, smelling of disinfectant and stale cigarettes. It was dark too, there were no windows in the grey metal walls. And on the floor, sitting carefully on newspapers, were three pale men in expensive suits. They didn't say anything, didn't look round. Hiller turned back to Salto on the pavement. He knew there was something wrong from his face. But it was too late now. The door was closed, and locked on the outside. It was out of Salto's hands.

They drove for an hour and a half and then they came to a
town. The van moved slowly through the traffic before
stopping outside a carpark. Hiller saw the red and white
barrier through the windscreen, saw it go up. Then the
Guv'nor drove on, and reversed into a gap.

It was a large carpark, the wind coming over a wide
clear space and booming against the metal walls. The men
in the back of the van were quiet now. For all their
expensive suits, Hiller knew they were small men. He'd
heard them talking earlier, and he knew why they were
here. One of them was a Photographer, and the other two
were John Smiths.

The Guv'nor turned from the wheel, his body bursting
out of his sweater. There was this anger about him that
never seemed far away. He was like every army corporal
Hiller had ever known. And he explained things like a corporal, in slow obsessive detail.

'You and you.' He pointed at Hiller and one of the John
Smiths. 'You get out of here and go across the carpark.
You get to the main street, you go down it to the right, and
halfway down you come to the bank.'

He was looking at Hiller now. 'And just remember
there's nothing to it. You go in with him, he does a cheque,
and he takes his time so you can have a look around. And
you're muckers, see? You talk a bit. Nothing in the world
to worry about. And once you seen what you want to see,
you come back here. Got that?'

Hiller nodded.

But when he got out of the van it all seemed unreal.
There were supermarket trollies rattling towards him over
the gravel. There were women with head-scarves, and
children trailing behind them. Hiller wondered what he
was doing as he walked after the John Smith.

A shopping arcade led away from the carpark. It was
bright, echoing to the sound of guitars and the clump of
high heels. Young girls wore the same huge boots as the

city girls but they bulged over the tops, and their coats were plastic and fake fur. The shop windows had more of the same. Radio-grams and jagged Odeon-style carpets were stacked up like fairground prizes. There was the smell of frying onions. And at the end of the arcade where the department stores began, a man was changing HUGE COOKER EVENT to VISIT SANTA'S CAVE.

It was a new town, new brick, new concrete, new cars. The High Street was wide, the sky bigger than in London, and the wind colder. Hiller turned up his collar as he walked past a Zebra Crossing and a Wimpy Bar. Then he stopped.

Facing him was a new white building, three storeys high. It had an alley on one side and an ironmonger's shop on the other. And over the doorway in gold letters it said NATIONAL GENERAL BANK.

Hiller followed the John Smith inside. It was warm suddenly, and larger than he'd expected. People moved quickly over a wide tiled floor, mosaic pillars glittered in the light from above, and the counter was long, of dark polished wood. There was the hum of air-conditioning, the smell of warm paint that comes from new radiators. It was like any other brand new bank.

Until Hiller counted the queues.

There were five of them. Which made it a Grade A Bank, built for the high cash flow of the late 1980s. And Hiller shivered in spite of the warmth. Because he knew the Guv'nor was being greedy.

'Come on.' The John Smith led him over to a writing table. He sat down and started making out a cheque.

But Hiller didn't see him any more. He didn't see any of the people in the bank, nor the bright walls. Instead he saw the steel behind the paint. The trembler-alarms set into the bricks and mortar, one every three metres. And the toughened steel mesh behind the frosted windows.

His hands were shaking as he turned away and looked up. And he saw it then, the chrome grille high up in the corner which had nothing to do with the air-conditioning, and which slid back at night. He saw the two machines behind the grille, the television camera and the VSU. The camera was small, the VSU large, a black wide-muzzled gun that shot out beams of ultra-sonic sound and scanned the reflections that came back. Hiller knew that the whole ground floor of this building had a dimension that wasn't marked on any architect's plan – a Volume Signature – calculated to within one cubic foot. At night, anything larger than a moving cat would disturb it. And a red light would flash on a monitor desk three miles away.

'That's it then.' The John Smith tore off the cheque and stood up. He led Hiller over to a queue. 'Did you see the big fight last night?'

'No,' Hiller said, 'I didn't.'

'That referee, he must have been blind. And the commentator, he was watching a different fight altogether.'

'Is that so?'

Hiller turned and looked at the counter. Again he saw the hidden steel. In this case, quarter inch steel, bullet-proof, behind the polished wood. And the glass, bullet-proof again, which stretched up to the ceiling where it was bolted to a girder that was an integral part of the structure . . .

'You didn't see the fight, then? You don't like boxing?'

'Oh, for Christ's sake,' Hiller said.

But the John Smith just smiled at him. 'Relax,' he said. 'It may never happen.'

And he was right. Hiller got hold of himself. He turned away from the counter and started doing the job he'd been sent here to do. He stared at the grey tiled floor, the white line which separated it from its black surround. He stared at the tables and chairs against the far wall, the waste paper baskets, the umbrella stand.

And then he saw what he wanted. Not one, but three of them, spaced out between the tables.

In the darkness of the van Hiller told the Guv'nor what he'd seen.

The Guv'nor turned to the Photographer. 'All right,' he said. 'Choose one of the three, the easiest one to work with, and get some pictures.'

The man nodded. He had a transistor radio in his hands. On the front of it was a large tuning knob with a flat mirror surface. A one-way mirror, Hiller saw. Because the top of the radio hinged back, showing the Nikon camera that was inside, screwed into the back of the glass.

'I want good, clear pictures. Front, sides, and top,' the Guv'nor said. 'And I want measurements and all. Because we're going to have to make one of the bleeding things up.'

'Okay.' The Photographer went to the rear of the van and got out.

The Guv'nor looked round at the second John Smith. 'Let's have you,' he said.

The John Smith moved up towards the grey light of the cab. He opened a briefcase and found a letter. 'I go along to this Estate Agent's, name of Hatherley's,' he said.

The Guv'nor nodded.

'I work for this Company, Rogers & Turnbull. And we're after offices in the town here. There's one in the High Street, one in Gladstone Street, and one in Archer's Road.'

'And which one are you after most?'

'The one in the High Street.'

'What else?'

'We're photo-printers,' the John Smith said. 'And we want Phase 3 electricity, and somewhere to pour chemicals down the drain. So we want the street plan with all the mains and services marked in.'

'And,' the Guv'nor gripped his arm, 'if they haven't got hold of that plan from the Town Hall, like you asked. Then you wait in their bloody office till they put it in your hand.'

'Right,' the John Smith said.

'On your way then.'

Forty minutes later he was back with a large roll of paper.

92

The Guv'nor spread it out on the front seat.

'Here we are.' He traced with his finger. 'Phone and power cables come along here, under this service road that runs behind the High Street. That's all right, isn't it?'

Then his finger stopped. 'What's this place? This place here?'

The John Smith leaned over the back of the seat. 'That's next to the bank, isn't it? That's Kramer's Yard. Garden machinery, Calor gas, stuff like that. It backs onto Kramer's Hardware shop in the High Street.'

The Guv'nor thought for a moment. 'That's it then. We can get at the underground cables from there. And we can move in from there. Nice and quiet of an evening.'

He turned to Hiller. 'This device of yours? How far away from the bank can it be worked?'

'Anything up to 300 yards,' Hiller said.

'And it doesn't matter about brick walls. Or any metal maybe that gets in the way?'

Hiller shook his head.

'All right.' The Guv'nor rolled up the paper. 'We visit Kramer's Yard tomorrow. We done enough for today.'

The next afternoon there were four of them in the van – the Guv'nor, the Photographer, Hiller, and a new John Smith. And behind them, by the rear doors, was an old rusty motor-mower.

It was raining. It drummed steadily on the metal roof, and the tyres hissed as they drove down the High Street. They turned left at the traffic lights, then left again into the service road.

'Now remember,' the Guv'nor said. 'You want the cylinder re-ground, you want the base-plate straightened, and a general overhaul.'

'I know,' the John Smith said. 'I had a mower done before.'

'Just get it right.'

The Guv'nor braked to a halt by some white gates. They were open onto a long gravelled yard. There was a lean-to on the left, where galvanised iron and rolls of chicken wire were stacked. And at the far end was a workshop, the flicker of a welding torch coming from its windows.

The John Smith and the Photographer got out of the van, swearing at the rain. They heaved the mower out, ran with it over to the workshop doors, and rang the bell. A man came out, a tall man with large oil-stained hands. He bent over the old machine a moment and shook his head. The John Smith pointed up at the rain, and they pushed the mower in through the doors.

Five minutes later the Photographer came out alone. He took pictures of the yard, and of the wall opposite the lean-to. It was the side wall of the National General Bank.

Then the John Smith came out. He was angry, and he still had the mower. The Photographer helped him haul it back to the van.

'Wouldn't he do it?' the Guv'nor asked as they got the mower inside.

'Wouldn't look at it. Said it was clapped out.'

'They don't want to know about anything old, do they?' the Guv'nor said. 'Bloody criminal.'

Then he slid out of the driving seat and signed to the John Smith to take over.

'You want me to drive?'

'I want you to take that mower back up the smoke and dump it.'

'What about you then?'

'Drop us off round the corner here,' the Guv'nor said. 'We're meeting a feller in a pub at seven o'clock. Him and me.' He pointed at Hiller.

'You mean I'm coming?' Hiller was alarmed.

The Prince's Bar was deserted, sad with muzak and cold PVC chairs. But the Guv'nor was at home, it was his territory. He bought the drinks, he got the evening paper from the barman, and he sat hunched up in his wet raincoat over the racing page.

Hiller was sweating. He drank the first Scotch quickly, and tried to slow up on the second. He knew the Guv'nor was counting.

Then they both turned. The door opened and a man came in, a small man with a suede jacket. He had fair wispy hair and a moustache that hardly showed in the dim light. The Stoppo Driver.

He bought a drink and came over. He and the Guv'nor talked for a while, talked about nothing. They seemed to be waiting.

Then the Stoppo looked at his watch. 'Should be clear by now,' he said.

Hiller followed the two of them outside. He shouldn't have been surprised by the Jaguar XJ6 parked at the kerb, but he was. He was surprised by the soft leather seat he sank into, by the sound the door made as it shut, and by the way the rain seemed suddenly far away. Then he saw the driving seat. It was lower than the passenger's seat, further forward, and bolted to the floor.

They drove through dark streets, going out of the town. They came to a trading estate where the factories were dim, surrounded by cold blue light. The Stoppo slowed up. He fastened his safety belt, and the Guv'nor did the same.

A gateway came up on the left. There were four Bedford vans parked behind it. Armoured vans. A sign said ALL NIGHT SECURITY LTD.

The Guv'nor clicked a stopwatch.

The Stoppo drove faster then. It didn't seem so. There were no howling tyres, no sudden slides on the wet roads. The gears he snatched quickly, but the rest of him was slow, holding the small racing wheel at arm's length, and moving it just enough each time. Hiller was surprised to see the speedometer flick up to 90 on three separate occasions. Then they came back into light, shopfronts shining on wet pavements. The streets were empty, and the Stoppo made sure, looking all round him and into his mirror. He slowed a little now, but he shot the traffic lights in the High Street at amber.

They passed the National General Bank. The Guv'nor clicked the stopwatch again. 'Four minutes, forty-seven,' he said.

The Stoppo took his foot off. 'They won't do it as quick as that, not in their Noddy vans. So you got six minutes, haven't you? Six minutes, top.'

'That'll do,' the Guv'nor said. 'That'll do fine.'

Both men relaxed then. They took off their safety belts and sat back. But behind them, Hiller was on the edge of his seat. His throat was dry. 'Why . . . ?' he began.

'Why what?' The Guv'nor turned.

'Why're you showing me all this?'

'Because you need to know.'

'But this afternoon, I mean? In Kramer's Yard?'

'You need to know Kramer's Yard too.'

'Why?'

'Because that's where you'll be working from.'

'*Working* from?' Hiller was frightened.

'You said you'd set the device up, show us how to work it.'

'But that doesn't have to be done at Kramer's Yard, for Christ's sake. It's Coppens who's going to be there, on the night.'

'Coppens isn't coming,' the Guv'nor said.

They were out of the town now, on a stretch of dual carriageway. 'Pull over.' The Guv'nor pointed at the verge.

The Stoppo parked and switched off. There was silence. And as he sat there in the warmth, in the rich blue glow of the dashboard, Hiller couldn't believe what was happening.

'What you got to understand about Coppens is he gets paid a lot of money,' the Guv'nor said. 'And he reckons we'd just be throwing it away this time.'

'But I thought he liked the idea. I thought he said it'd work.'

'Oh, that? He reckons it'll work all right, reckons the

alarms can be fixed, no trouble at all.'

'Well, then?'

'What he said was . . . Where's the point in the priciest Bellman in London coming along just to do a TV repair job?'

'A what?'

'Taking care of the closed circuit TV. He said anyone could do that. Even you.'

And Hiller understood then, why Coppens had asked him about the TV cable.

'He said it was easy.' The Guv'nor leaned towards him.

Hiller didn't answer.

'It is easy, isn't it?'

Hiller backed away. But not quickly enough. The Guv'nor grabbed his shirt.

'Isn't it?'

'Yes,' he had to admit it.

'Well, then,' the Guv'nor let him go. 'You come with us on the night. You take care of the alarms and the TV. From Kramer's Yard. And that's before we even think of going in the bank. So where's your bother?'

The next morning Hiller was due to go into the bank again. Through the front door, in opening hours.

There were four of them in the Jaguar – the Guv'nor, the Stoppo, the Donkey, and Hiller. They were moving slowly down the High Street when the Guv'nor turned. 'You're on your own this time. We didn't bring a John Smith.'

He got a cheque-book from his pocket. 'The top one's already made out. It's good, there's money to meet it. And there's a cheque-card in the back.'

Hiller took it from him.

The Guv'nor moved closer. Again he explained things in slow careful detail: 'Now you go in there, you find an empty table, and you make as if you're writing the cheque, like this, so no-one can see. Then you sit there and you light a fag or something. You're waiting, see? Until there's

97

a clear space around you, and you can do your thing with the suitcase.'

Hiller nodded.

The car stopped near the bank, and they let him out. He got the suitcase from the boot, and he handled it carefully. There was delicate machinery inside, even if it was held together by bits of Meccano. As he walked over to the bank he held the case low, so that no-one could see the cut-out in the bottom.

He went into the warmth and the bright light again. But he saw only the table to his left, the one at the end that was free. He sat down there and pretended to make out the cheque, as the Guv'nor had said. Then he looked round. There was no-one else near him. He stood up, cheque-book and pen in one hand, suitcase in the other. He took two steps towards the counter and appeared to change his mind. Because he put the suitcase down, put his pen in his pocket, and kept the cheque-book out. And as he bent to pick up the suitcase again, he pressed a small bulge at one end of its handle. Inside the case, a light-meter got a reading from the black tiles at the floor's edge, and a stylus recorded it on paper.

He hesitated twice more on his way to the counter, and got two more readings from the floor. Then he went over to the cashier.

'Thank you, sir.' The man took his cheque, cheque-book, and card. He looked at the name, and then reached for the duds-list at his side.

Hiller waited. But the cheque was good, as the Guv'nor had said.

'How would you like it, Mr Dallas, sir?'

'As it comes,' Hiller said.

'Ten . . . Twenty . . . Twenty-five . . .'

And then Hiller saw past him, past the clerk's desks and the filing cabinets to the lift door in the corner. It was steel, it had a diamond-shaped window, and it had no door-handle. There were just two keyholes, five feet apart, one on each side of the door.

Hiller's hands started to shake.

'Is there anything wrong, sir?'

He snatched up the money and ran.

Back in the car, the Guv'nor saw his face. 'What's up?'

'That's an AA Graded bank,' Hiller shouted. 'That's the highest grade there is outside of London and Birmingham.'

'Get away,' the Guv'nor said.

'How many of them d'you think there are, for Christ's sake? They're specials, aren't they? Geared up to deal with bloody great cash-flows over the next ten years. There are going to be bloody great factories around here, bloody great stores . . .'

'. . . Not going to be,' the Guv'nor cut in. 'They're here right now.'

'An AA Graded *bank*,' Hiller shouted again. 'There's only one entrance to that strong-room. And that's through a lift with solid steel walls. The whole damn strong-room complex is like a box of steel inside the building.'

'All right. All right.'

'But there's another thing, isn't there?' Hiller was pale suddenly. 'There's a second TV set-up in there, inside that steel box. And you have to go in there, up in that lift to deal with it. *I* have to go in there to . . .'

He reached out for the door handle.

The Donkey grabbed him, pulled his jacket down, pinning his arms.

'Get going,' the Guv'nor said.

They parked in a narrow lane out in the country. The Donkey pushed Hiller through a gate into a stubbled field. 'Lie down and keep still.' He held a baseball bat in both hands.

Hiller lay down. The stubble was wet. Slimy black leaves had fallen from the tree overhead.

The Guv'nor came in through the gate. He had a shot-gun. He came over to Hiller and knelt down. 'Keep your legs *straight*.'

And it was his voice, out of control. It wasn't the same man.

He moved suddenly. He jammed the shotgun up Hiller's trouser-leg, tearing the cloth, tearing the skin.

'Listen,' he was sweating, his face mottled and strange, 'I know of three other people who'll come into the bank and do the TV job for me. *Three* of them.'

He shoved the gun barrels hard up into Hiller's crutch. Hiller gasped.

'But the first one, I don't like, see? And the second one's inside. And the third, he's away spending money in Spain.'

His thumb squeezed off the safety catch.

'And I could wait till he gets back. Only I don't want to. I want to pull this fugging bank while the fugging Christmas money's there. *Got* it?'

The barrels dug into Hiller's crutch again. The pain was bad. His head came up. Then it stopped. Because of that safety catch.

'So that leaves you, doesn't it? And if you can do a TV job outside the bank, you can do it inside. I keep hearing it's easy.'

Hiller waited for the barrels to come up again. But they didn't. For a moment the Guv'nor was quite still. Then he started to shake.

'Say no,' he said. 'Go on, say bloody no.'

The shaking got worse.

And the Guv'nor's left hand came up to shield his face. From the blast. He wanted the shaking to get to the trigger. Just wanted the excuse.

'All *right*,' Hiller shouted.

19

In the dawn light Hiller sat watching the sleeping boy. He'd sat like that for some time, ever since they'd brought him back to the flat. He hadn't moved, hadn't even bothered to take off his raincoat. He'd just watched the boy and drunk from the Scotch bottle.

And why he was drinking was because there was a thick roll of notes in his pocket, the insurance money Salto had given him. And he wasn't going to use it.

Because the last time he'd gone on the run he'd had £500, and Salto had found him in a fortnight.

And now it wasn't Salto he had to deal with any more. It was the Guv'nor.

Hiller took another pull from the bottle. His face was grey and stubbled, his eyes red-rimmed. He felt his thigh where the trousers were torn, where they were caked with blood.

Behind him the door opened. Mo came in, pale in a long flowered nightdress.

' 'lo,' she said.

Hiller didn't turn. Mechanically he slid the bottle behind him and felt in his pocket for peppermints.

'Why've you got your coat on indoors?'

He didn't answer.

'Why have you?'

'Oh.' He made the effort. 'I think you have to wear a coat every now and then, in case you forget how.'

She nodded.

He found the bag of peppermints and put one in his mouth.

'Connive one?'

He handed them to her.

'I only came in for a chap,' she said. She was trying to help him out.

'That's good,' he said dully. 'What shall we chap about?'

'I don't know. What's your best?'

'My best what?'

'Your best anything.'

'Well, mostly it's ice cream.' He felt sick at the thought of it.

'What flavour?'

'Sausage flavour.' He felt sicker. 'Sausage flavour ice cream.'

'That's not bad.' She lowered her voice. 'And d'you know what his best is?' She was pointing at the boy.

Hiller turned once again and stared at the small grey head on the pillow. Stared for a long time. He was thinking about the Guv'nor, his finger on the trigger. 'Yes,' he said finally, 'I know what his best is.'

'Why d'you say it like that?'

'Oh . . .'

She came closer, frowning. 'His best,' she said. 'I mean, he says his best is a toy boat that goes on the water. It goes left and right, backwards and forwards, all on its own.'

'Oh, that?'

She touched his arm. 'But there isn't a boat like that, is there? Not one that goes left and right, backwards and forwards, all on its own? By magic?'

'I'm afraid there is.' And Hiller sighed. Because if you knew how to work the boat, it could also get you into the National General Bank. By magic.

He looked round at Mo then and saw her for the first time, the way she was twisting her hands.

'What's the matter?'

'Well, he . . .' she nodded again at the boy '. . . he says the boat's his best. And that's why you're going to buy it for him.'

102

And he understood. 'All right,' he said, 'why don't you tell me what your best is too?'

'No.'

'Come on.'

She didn't want to, but finally it was too much for her: 'It's a trike. A red trike called a Racer. It's got a basket on the front and on the back, and it's in a shop.'

Hiller smiled at her red face, her shame. He felt in his pocket for the thick roll of banknotes, the money Salto had given him. And suddenly he knew what it was for.

Gort went out with him later in the morning. They took a taxi to Hamley's in Regent Street, and went up to the top floor.

Hiller saw it then, the cabin cruiser. It had a blue hull, a shiny white deck, and it was two feet long.

'Can I see it working?' he asked the assistant.

The man was grey-haired. He had bacon and a suburban train-ride on his breath, and he caught the smell of whisky on Hiller's. 'I'm afraid this is our busy time of the year,' he said. 'We can't really demonstrate it, in the crush.'

'Is it the radio-controlled one?' Hiller was angry.

'Yes, but . . .'

'. . . How much?'

'£139.90.'

'I'll take two of them.' Hiller peeled off fifteen £20 notes. 'Just wrap them up.'

'Batteries are extra,' the man said sourly.

Gort watched him go away. 'Why are you getting two?' he asked.

Hiller lowered his voice. 'One to make up the device,' he said. 'And one for the boy.'

With the two parcels under his arm, he led the way on to the cycle department. He found the red trike that was called a Racer and bought it for Mo. The assistant wrapped it in corrugated cardboard, leaving the wheels free. And Gort pushed it out onto the pavement.

They went down Regent Street, looking for a taxi. Passers-by stared at Hiller's torn trousers flapping round his leg. He stopped outside the windows of Austin Reed. Then he went in. He bought a dark blue shantung suit, a silk shirt, a tie, socks, and underwear. He had a shave and a haircut in the basement.

And by the time they got back to Salto's flat, he'd spent £682.

'Wait a minute.' He locked the bedroom door while he hid the second cabin cruiser under the bed. Then he let the children in.

'That's for you.' He helped Mo untie the string and tear away the cardboard wrapping. She stared at the tricycle, the stick-of-rock redness of it, the shiny handlebars with their white grips. And for a moment she was afraid. Then she got onto the saddle. Hiller had just a brief glimpse of her face as she pedalled out of the room, but it was enough. For the life of him he couldn't understand why adults made children say thank you.

Then he saw the boy with the boat. It was big. Big enough for him to lay his cheek against the hull and be in the cockpit. And he was pale, owning everything he saw there. The blue seat cushions, the hatchway leading down to the cabin below, the chrome wheel, and the manikin in the yachting cap who was holding it.

'Radio controlled,' Hiller said. 'Left and right rudder, forward and reverse engines, and the searchlight.'

He fitted the aerial to the cabin top. Then he got out the radio control handset. It was a blue plastic box, the size of a shaver. It also had an aerial and three control stalks.

Hiller went out. He went down the hall to the front door. Then he pushed the first control stalk forward.

And in the bedroom, fifty feet away, the boat suddenly whirred in the boy's hands. The propellers spun round, stopped, then went into reverse. A moment later the searchlight came on, throwing a white circle of light on the wall. Finally the rudder turned. And the manikin holding the wheel turned with it, seeming to steer the boat.

The boy's eyes were soft and far away.

Hiller came back into the room and gave him the handset. 'It's an expensive toy,' he said. 'I know you'll take care of it.'

The boy nodded and went out. Hiller slumped back on the bed, the whisky catching up with him.

Then there was a knock on the door. Anna came in with the tricycle, her mouth was tight.

'I can't let Mo take this,' she said.

'You can't what?' He was too tired to understand.

'It's too much money.'

'Oh, come on . . .'

'. . . And there's another thing. I mean, Mo told you. About this trike called a Racer. The one she wanted.'

'No,' he said. 'It was the first one I saw in the shop.'

'You couldn't lie to a two-year-old.' She came towards him. 'Look, I don't care if you have to bribe your kid all the time.'

'Bribe?'

'That's right. Those toys he's got. They weren't cheap, were they? And that insane pocket money deal you've got with him. I heard all about it.'

Hiller backed away.

'I don't care,' she said. 'It's not my business. But I'm not having you going out and spending a fortune on Mo.'

'It's only money.'

'What?'

'Moneyah.' And suddenly he was angry, strangely American-angry in his shiny suit. 'For Christ's sake, people go *on* and *on* telling you that's what makes the world go round. And you don't believe them . . . And then one day, misery, you find it's true.' He pulled the remaining £20 notes from his pocket. 'Moneyah. And there's a lot more where that came from. A few grand, that's what they call it, isn't it? And they're pushing it my way because suddenly it seems I'm useful to them.'

She looked at the money. Then she looked on, at the

new suit, the silk shirt, the tie. And her face was strange.

'I bought Mo the trike because I wanted to get her something nice,' Hiller said. 'That's all.'

'But there's another side to it.'

'Maybe there is. Maybe I'm wrong.' He looked down at the shiny red frame, the handlebars. 'But you can't take it away from her now? Can you?'

Anna hesitated. Behind her the door was open. She could hear Mo crying in the kitchen.

'Go on.' Hiller turned the trike round and pushed it back to her.

And finally she nodded. 'But it's not just Mo that's crying,' she said. 'It's your kid too. He wants to go out to the park with his boat. And Salto won't let him.'

'Send him in here,' Hiller said.

'The boy?'

'No. Salto.'

She stared at him.

Hiller was filling his pipe when Salto came in. He felt a hand take the tobacco tin from him. Then he was picked up suddenly by his shirtfront and sat on a chair.

Salto looked down at him. And Hiller had remembered only the man in the dirty jeans, wheeling and dealing on the phone. He hadn't remembered his height, his dark tired eyes, his strength.

'Hi, Hearty.' Salto unwrapped a cigar. 'Like the suit, the shirt. Very nice.'

Hiller didn't answer.

'You're all the same, aren't you? Get mixed up in a racket, get fourpence, and you flash it around . . . And why? Because you're scared out of your tiny mind.' He held out the cigar. 'Got a match?'

Hiller gave him a box. He sat there, his new suit crumpling around him.

Salto walked away. He lit the cigar, taking his time.

'All right,' Hiller said finally. 'I'm scared. And you know why, don't you?'

106

Salto nodded.

'For Christ's sake, why didn't you tell me about the bank? About Coppens not wanting to take the job?'

'They didn't want me to tell you,' Salto said. 'It's not me running the show any more. You know that, don't you?'

He came back and stood close to Hiller. 'Look, Heart, I'll play fair with you. I've always played fair with you, haven't I? . . . Okay, your cut's going to be forty grand, not twenty. Quids, in a Swiss Bank. And that's still cheap for a job of this size.'

Hiller looked round at the torn wrappings in the room, the paper that had covered the cabin cruiser, and the cardboard that had covered the trike. 'Will it make any difference?' he asked. 'Forty or twenty?'

'It will later,' Salto said. 'Believe me.'

He chewed on the end of his cigar a moment. 'And if I were you, I'd get to work on that trick device of yours. These boys are in a hurry. They want to move right away.'

Hiller sighed. 'Does it have to be today? I need some sleep. And then I wanted to take the kids out to the park.'

'All right.' Salto nodded.

'All right, what?'

'I'll tell them you've got the day off.'

'Why?' Hiller was surprised.

'Because I don't like them, dear Heart. And I like you more the way you are right now.'

'What d'you mean?'

Salto stood Hiller up. He smoothed the shantung suit around him and straightened his tie. 'Remember the way you came in here? Your shirt ripped to pieces, those tatty suitcases . . . and, what was it, Sod's Law?'

That afternoon Sod's Law seemed very far away. They went out to the park, Hiller in his new suit, and Anna in a good woollen coat that he hadn't seen before. They were walking slowly in the direction of the pond, when a uniformed nanny came towards them along the path. She saw the way they were dressed, she saw the children's new toys, and she nodded at them. Just for a moment in her eyes they were a family, of the right sort.

And there was another moment – a much more real moment – later when it was getting dark. The cabin cruiser was out on the pond. The manikin in the yachting cap was docking it slowly, edging backwards and forwards, turning the wheel. Suddenly the searchlight cut through the dusk, finding the crowd of children at the water's edge. And they were silent, knowing it was magic.

The boy stood above them, working the controls. His face was thin and finely tuned. Because he knew it was magic too, but of the most powerful sort – magic that had been given to him.

When he got back to the flat, Hiller locked himself in the bedroom. And he started to work on the device.

There were small pieces of machinery in front of him, the parts of the toy he'd made a week ago – the tortoise.

He turned and got another toy from under the bed. It was the second cabin cruiser, the one he'd kept hidden from the boy. He took it out of its box and split it into two pieces with a screwdriver. And he removed the mechanism from inside.

Then he looked at what he'd done. The cockpit of the cruiser was now lying upside down, its blue seats, its manikin hidden. Just a dull white piece of plastic on the floor.

20

Two afternoons later, Hiller sat in a car parked in the West End. He had a radio control handset on his knees, and a stopwatch.

The handset was a small blue box, the same as the boy's. Except that two of the three control stalks had been removed. And in one of the empty sockets there was a torch bulb.

Hiller switched on. He pushed the control stalk forwards and watched the bulb. It began to flicker, slowly at first, but then more quickly until it became a steady light. When that happened, Hiller started the watch.

He kept the control stalk pressed forwards for 80 seconds before he switched off. Then he pulled the stalk back, switched on again, and re-started the watch. In another 80 seconds it was all over. As simple as that.

He put the handset and watch away, and got out of the car. The sounds of a market came down the street towards him. He walked past the rows of stalls and came to the alley with the strip club. The pub doorway was opposite. He went up the dark stairs, ignoring the noise from the Saloon Bar.

The dance floor upstairs was deserted. Hiller stood quite still a moment. There were two things that caught his eye. The first was a pile of thick white insulation tape. A large pile. Someone had been using a lot of tape.

And the second was the device.

It was there, staring him in the face. But no-one would see it in the National General Bank, no-one would give it a second glance. Because the mechanism was hidden now, installed in one of the three objects he'd seen that morning in the bank. Not one of the original three. A fourth had been made up in a metal workshop, using the Photographer's pictures.

'Over here.'

Hiller turned. It took him a moment to see the Guv'nor. The room was dark, a forest of paper chains and tinsel hung down from the ceiling, obscuring what little light there was.

Behind the Guv'nor other men were standing in the shadows. There were five of them – Salto, the Stoppo, the Donkey, the Peterman, and the Peterman's Donkey.

'All right,' The Guv'nor turned to them, 'He did it, didn't he' He was 300 bleeding yards away down the street, and he did it like he said. You all saw that.'

The men stared at Hiller as if they didn't believe what they'd seen.

He went towards them.

'And he does the same thing on the night,' the Guv'nor said. 'From outside the bank, from Kramer's Yard. That's how he works the false alarms.'

They nodded.

'Now, you all know what happens then,' the Guv'nor went on. 'But I'll go over it again, because it's important . . . First off, a red light comes on in the Noddy Station, see? Then the Noddy Men turn up at the bank in their van. They go in, check the place out, and find it's a false alarm. So they lock up again and go away. And they switch off that red light.'

He paused, looking round. 'But they can only do that three times, can't they? Because the fourth time they can't switch off that red light no more. It comes on and it stays on. So the alarms are blown, the building's wide open. And that means the Noddy Men are going to turn up at the bank with their camp beds and hot water bottles. They're going to kip down on the ground floor.'

'Which is when we go in,' the Stoppo said. 'We cut our way into the Strong Room from upstairs.'

'It would be,' the Guv'nor told him. 'Except we're doing an AA Graded Bank. The big one.'

Nobody spoke as he turned away. Then they followed him, over to the bandstand at the end of the room.

It was hung with balloons and streamers, a large banner said HAPPY XMAS & A PROSPEROUS NEW YEAR. And underneath it, pinned to the floor of the stage, was a town street plan.

'The National General Bank, New Morley.' The Guv'nor pointed to it. 'The outside walls here've got the usual stuff. Trembler alarms, wired doors and windows. . . . And right here in the middle of the building

110

there's the Security Area.' He drew a small black square. 'Nobody's going to cut their way in there. There's too many steel walls before you get to the Strong Room . . . There's only one way in, see? And that's through the lift doors on the ground floor.'

'Ground floor?' The Donkey stared at him. 'But that's where the Noddy Men's going to be.'

'Right. So we got to be in through those lift doors *before* the Noddy Men move in for the night.'

'For Christ's sake, they're going to be all round us.'

'So what?' The Guv'nor shrugged. 'How're they going to know we're in that lift shaft? They can't tell nothing from the alarms. They can't see us in there. And they can't hear us through four inches of steel.'

'No,' the Donkey said. 'No, I see that.' But he didn't see.

'It's like this,' the Guv'nor told him. 'When that red light's on, the building's wide open, like I said . . . And it comes on four times in all, including the last time when the Noddy Men move in. So how long's it on for each time?'

'I dunno.'

'Six minutes,' the Stoppo said.

'Right.' The Guv'nor nodded. 'It takes six minutes for the Noddy van to reach the bank each time. So that's four lots of six minutes, which is twenty-four minutes.' He turned away. 'And that's time enough for us to open a few doors, isn't it, Nob?'

Another man moved into the light from the bandstand. The Peterman. He was short and frail, with elevated shoes that made strange creases in his trousers. He opened a briefcase, and as he bent over it his hair came away from his collar, leaving a sudden thin neck. 'Easy,' he said. 'Easy. We could do it in half the time.'

He got out a loose-leaf file and found a page. Hiller saw it was one of the pages he'd copied from the Print-Out.

'We reckon to go in the back door, don't we?' the Peterman asked.

'That's it.'

'Two bolts, two locks.' The man's finger stopped half-

111

way down the page. 'The locks are Sanger's, magno-jobs. And they put them in . . . August 84 . . . So that gives them a serial number between 2350 and 2425, prefix AQ.'

'And the lock on the lift doors?'

'Sanger's again. And it's a big one. Three-input, coded key job, tailor-made. . . . That's a bit more tricky. But it went in there September '84 . . . Nothing to worry about.'

'So we practically got keys for the bloody building.'

The talk went on. Then the Guv'nor hauled himself up onto the bandstand. He looked down at the rest of them. 'Any questions?'

The man next to Hiller was uneasy, he'd been uneasy a long time. He was a heavily built man, the Peterman's Donkey. 'Yes,' he said. 'You keep saying *van*. When the Noddy *van* turns up at the bank.'

'What d'you mean?'

'What happens if they send two vans? I mean, that'd double it up, wouldn't it?'

'It would,' the Guv'nor said. 'Only they won't send two vans. They won't have one spare.'

'Why's that?'

'Because Nob here, he's got hold of some black plastic stuff called Eversoft.'

'You mean, the IRA stuff?'

'That's it. There's going to be a little bang on the other side of town. Car bomb. That'll keep any spare Noddy patrols busy. And the Law.'

'What if someone gets hurt?'

'They won't. There'll just be a hole in the road,' the Guv'nor said. 'The car's parked outside an empty building, isn't it? Council offices, Town Hall, anywhere with a coat of arms on it. That's all those fugging Micks need.'

The man nodded.

'That answer your question?'

'Yes.'

But the Guv'nor stared at him. 'No, it doesn't,' he said.

112

'Does it?' He came down from the bandstand. 'What's up?'

'Well . . . There's something you left out, isn't there?'

'What's that?'

'The TV repair jobs. There's the one outside, in Kramer's Yard. And that's all right.'

'And?'

'Well, the other one. It's up at the top of the lift shaft, right inside the place.'

'It's the same as the first job. No difference.'

'But he's never been in a place before, has he?' The man turned. He was looking at Hiller.

'He's all right.'

'He may be that too. It's just I don't *know* him.'

The Guv'nor was quite still for a moment. Then he reached out for the man's shoulders. 'And you don't know us,' he said. 'You don't know this room, what we was talking about, or nothing.' He turned him round. 'On your way.'

The man's heels clicked away across the dance floor. The Guv'nor waited for the door to close. He was angry.

'Let's get it straight,' he said. 'How was it the other times? When we took Coppens? . . . I mean, Coppens is old. We took him in the place, we carried his bags, we showed him where to put his feet. Then we sat him down by the cables and he did the job. Isn't that right?'

The others nodded.

'Well, then.' The Guv'nor turned back to the Peterman. 'That was your sodding mate that walked out, wasn't it? So who we going to get to do your Donkey-work now? Help you out?'

'Doesn't matter much, does it?'

'We don't want some scruff who'll shoot his mouth off. It has to be somebody tight. . . Anybody got any ideas?'

There was no answer.

Then Salto spoke, for the first time: 'What about Gort? He's been in it from the beginning. And he's tight.'

'Gorty.' The Guv'nor nodded. 'Why not? He's done the

113

work before. . . How about it, Nob?'

'Gort'll do,' the Peterman said.

'That's it, then.' The Guv'nor folded up the street plan. 'There's just one more feller to see, and then we're finished here.'

'Someone else?' Salto was surprised. 'Who else is there?'

'Friend of yours,' the Guv'nor said. 'He's coming round here.'

Hiller sat where he'd been told to, behind a pile of folding chairs. There was just the light from the bandstand, and beyond it a table where the Guv'nor sat with the Peterman and Salto.

The Christmas decorations stirred as the door opened. A man came in from the shadows.

Hiller didn't see his face. He saw only the white shirt front and the gleam of the silk tie.

'We done business before, haven't we?' the Guv'nor said.

'I believe we have.' The Broker's voice was big-jowled, middle-aged.

'All I wanted to say,' the Guv'nor frowned. 'was that this time it's an awful lot of money.'

'Oh, I wouldn't say that.'

'I would. Yes, I would.'

The Broker shifted uneasily. 'You want to be sure. That's what you mean, is it?'

The Guv'nor waited, for the man's scent, his cigar-smell to fade a little. 'The money's going to get clear,' he said then. 'Two cars leave that bank. One with us, one with the money, same as always.. . . *We* take the tricky route because we got the good driver, same as always. . . The money takes the quick route, and gets put in a Swiss Bank by your mob, same as always. . . And if we're put inside or not, the account-numbers and the depositors' names get phoned to our mutual friend, same as always.'

'You don't need to worry on that score. It's quite . . .'

The Broker stopped, the jowl gone from his voice.

'That's good,' the Guv'nor said quietly. 'That's what I like to hear.'

There was a tiny squeal somewhere inside the Broker. He backed away.

'Would you say I was an old-fashioned man?' the Guv'nor asked.

'Never given it much thought, actually.'

'Ain't she sweet? Just a walkin' down the street?' the Guv'nor sang out of tune. 'Remember that one? Old fashioned?'

Suddenly he moved. Hiller didn't see what it was. Except there was liquid on the table. And smoke, as the Broker jerked his legs away.

Then he did see it. The hole where the centre of the table had been. The smell of bad eggs.

'An old-fashioned man,' the Guv'nor repeated. 'And if our mutual friend doesn't get phoned that that money's deposited, all of it, when you say it is. . . Then you'd better worry as you sit back drinking your Château-bottled Dooly-Hassen-Basser. You got that?'

The Broker was trembling.

After he'd gone, the Guv'nor got up. 'When's it going to be then, Nob?'

'I don't know. Has to be a Wednesday for the wages, doesn't it?' The Peterman shrugged. 'This week or next week.'

'That's what I thought.'

'But Wednesday, that's tomorrow.' Salto's voice was shaky.

'So?' The Guv'nor turned to him. 'We're all ready here. The Stoppo cars are ready, the van's ready, the Link-Men are ready. It's all wrapped up.'

He walked out to the shadows of the dance floor.

'I say it's tomorrow,' he said then. 'There's too many on the pay-roll, small fellers, bits and pieces. Leave them a week, and they're going to talk.'

The Peterman nodded.

But Salto was still shaky. 'Look, it's December. Why not wait a couple of weeks until the mail gets snarled up? And the banks have to take over the money side of . . .'

'. . . Christ, I learned it at fifteen.' The Guv'nor was angry. 'Seaside banks in August. Town banks in December, because of the Higher Value Packages.' He moved back towards the Peterman. 'Anyway that's peanuts, isn't it? Seeing as how we're going for an AA Graded Bank?'

'That's right.'

There was a long pause.

'How much money they got in there this Wednesday, Nob?'

The Peterman opened his loose-leaf file. He found the page in Hiller's handwriting. 'Wednesday 5 December,' he read. 'Cash Holding, £12,875,000 . . . estimated.'

'Wednesday it is then,' the Guv'nor said. 'Tomorrow.'

21

Hiller got back to the flat at seven in the evening. He sat on the window-sill in the kitchen, listening to the panes rattling, the gusts of wind coming over the dark city roofs. And suddenly his hands began to shake.

It was warm in the kitchen, but he couldn't feel it. The children were over by the electric fire, a red glow on their faces as they dried their hair after a bath. And Hiller wanted to be part of it. He hid his hands behind his back and went over.

'How's it going?' he asked the boy.

'All right.'

'How's the boat?'

'Smashing.' The boy was serious. He had the cabin

cruiser by his side. He took it with him everywhere he went.

'Did you get to the park again this afternoon?'

'Yeh.'

'And the batteries aren't run down yet?'

'She got me some more.'

And that wasn't all Anna had done for him. There were the new red and white pyjamas, the soft washed hair, the smell of toothpaste. Hiller remembered how long it had been since he'd put the boy to bed.

'How about a game?' he asked. 'Any game you like.'

'There's no time.' Mo rocked backwards and forwards on her chair. 'It's our story.'

'Oh?' Hiller turned to her. 'What one's that?'

'Grey Starling.'

'And it's good.' The boy surprised him. 'There's this place where they didn't think to put a lighthouse, and where a ship gets wrecked. And Grey Starling gets her dad's rowing boat and goes there and rescues eight people. That's all there was on the ship.'

'I know the one,' Hiller said.

He walked away and sat down at the table.

In a moment they went out, the three of them. Their voices came from the room next door. And then just Anna's voice, reading.

Hiller got up and went to his own room. He got the whisky from the wardrobe and took it back to the kitchen. He poured a glass and drank it quickly, but it didn't stop his hands shaking. He pushed the bottle away. He couldn't afford to get involved with that. Not tonight.

Anna came back, carrying the mugs that had held the children's milk. 'They're asleep,' she said. She moved easily, in faded jeans and sweater. And there was a calm about her Hiller hadn't seen before.

'Your boy,' she smiled at him, 'he's really nice, isn't he? Once you get to know him?'

'Yes,' Hiller said.

'You're very lucky.'

'Yes.'

'What's the matter?'

And then she saw the whisky bottle. Her mouth tightened. 'D'you want some food? There's half a chicken somewhere, and some slaw.'

'That'd be nice.'

'Pass us those plates then.'

They chattered as he put them down on the sideboard.

'For Christ's sake,' she swung round, 'd'you have to keep yourself stoked up on that stuff?'

'It's not the Scotch.'

'What is it then?'

'It's just my hands. They won't keep still.'

And then, as she stared at him strangely, he had to say it:

'You see, It's tomorrow . . . when we go out to do this thing.'

It took her a moment to understand. 'When *we* go out? You mean, you're going too?'

'There's something they want me to do. Something technical.'

She turned away.

'You stupid bastard,' she said then. Her voice was quite cold.

'Yes.'

'It's the money, isn't it?'

'No.' He shook his head.

'Oh, come on. That morning you were shooting your mouth off. All those grands that were coming your way.'

'It's not the money.'

'For Christ's sake.'

'Ask Salto,' he said. 'Ask him about the time he told me I was going to get £40,000, in a Swiss Bank.' He looked round at the bare white kitchen, 'It's too much. £5.99 for a gramophone record I can understand, £7.50 for a bottle of Scotch. But not forty thousand. Too many noughts.'

She turned back. And she saw it was true. She saw it from the new suit that was crumpled around him, the burns and solder marks, the grease where he'd held metal against his stomach.

'All right, if it isn't the money, what is it?'

He didn't answer.

'They put the frighteners on you, didn't they?' There was disgust on her face. 'You didn't know what you were tangling with, and they marked you, smacked you around.'

'No, it's not that either.' He was speaking softly now, standing quite firm. Only his hands were shaking. 'You see, there's a limit to the amount of fear you can feel. All right, there's a moment each time when they take off their coats. But after that, the knives, the fists, the shotguns even . . . They're all happening to someone else. I don't expect you'd know.'

And she saw that was true as well. For the first time she saw the hardness behind his slack chin, behind his eyes.

'I could've got out any time . . . on my own,' he said. 'But in the end there was only one thing to do. I decided that.'

'*You* decided?'

'That's right. A couple of days ago when Mo came into my room, early in the morning. She asked me what the boy's best was.'

'The boy's what?'

'His best thing.' He looked straight at her. 'And I didn't tell her, but I knew what the boy's best was that morning. It was staying alive.'

Suddenly she was afraid.

'Yes . . . It was all right, you see, until this afternoon. My bloody hands . . . I mean, what chance have I got of doing a job tomorrow? And getting back here? With these?'

For a long moment she stared at his hands.

Then she turned and went out.

Hiller didn't understand. He reached out for the whisky and started drinking again. He heard Anna moving around next door. And he heard the wind battering against the window, getting stronger.

Then she came back into the room, wearing her overcoat.

'Are you going out?' He was surprised.

'No.'

And he knew she wasn't as she came over. It was just a beige woollen coat, but it was the way she was wearing it, the way she moved. Suddenly he knew what Gort had meant, about South Africa and the Bahamas.

She took the drink out of his hand and stood close to him. Her coat fell open. She was wearing two pieces of clothing underneath. They were loose, lace-trimmed, and there was the richness of Bond Street about them. Until she took something from her coat pocket.

It was a small bottle. She opened it and cupped her hand. There was the smell of scent as she oiled herself, around and on her clothing. Her small breasts came through the cloth, hard and shiny. Then her belly and on down, showing herself there. Finally she cupped her hand again. She oiled her mouth and then her tongue. She was standing over him, blotting out the light.

Her bedroom was heavy with the scent, strange and slightly sour the deeper he got into it. He saw Mo's bed was empty. Then he turned his back to undress.

As he got into bed he saw the hollows, the hard muscles of her thighs. Her whole body was hard, gleaming, a tool. And he was ugly and sweating. He hung back.

'Why?' he asked.

'Don't worry about it. I want to help you. The way I can.'

She switched out the light and began to work on him. But again the unease returned.

'Will it help if I tell you about some other men?' Her mouth was close to him.

'No.'

'That's not what I meant.' She was angry suddenly. 'For Christ's sake, what are you afraid of? These men were ten, twenty years older than you, They'd spend twelve-hundred quid just to get a hard-on.'

Her anger grew. Her thighs locked tight around him. 'Jesus, when you get to that level . . . novelty plays a certain part in it . . . to say the bloody least. . . . They just want to switch off . . . and become a thing . . . It's strange how excited . . . they get about that .. . .'

She was pumping down on him, bringing him near the edge. He tried to shut his ears. '. . . I nearly . . . killed a man once . . . He asked me . . . to nearly . . . kill him . . . *Je*-sus.'

She forced it out of him. And then she sank back, trembling.

Later it was as if the anger had gone out of her. She slept, with one arm looped across him. And later still she was soft. And he moved on top of her, deep into that warm apron of her that was soft the harder he had to crush it. And suddenly for him it was so strong. It opened his head and brought him shadows on a summerhouse wall, the sound of the sea, when he was nineteen.

He pleased her, or she let him think that. Either way it was enough. He felt close to her. The thin eggshell of her head was tight against his own.

But again he had to ask it:

'Why?'

And she gave a strange answer:

'Mo,' she said. 'The time she came from, it was very bad for me.'

'What d'you mean?'

'Men, mostly.'

'But I never understood,' he said. 'I mean, why . . . ?'

'. . . Why I had Mo?'

He nodded. 'I know it's none of my business. But a girl like you, she'd know how to . . . prevent that sort of thing, wouldn't she?'

'That's right.'

He awoke to daylight suddenly, and the sound of voices. Anna was over by the locked door, shouting through it to

Mo: 'Look, please go away. I'll be out in a second.'

'You said that before.'

'Go *away*.'

Mo went.

Anna turned back quickly. 'You'll have to get out of here, right now . . . No . . .' she couldn't make up her mind '. . . Get dressed first. And I'll go out and see if it's clear.'

He got out of bed and went to get his shirt. He saw the rooftops outside, the grey sky.

And then he remembered what day it was.

'Come on. Get dressed. Please.'

He reached out for his shirt. And it was only when he was buttoning it, that he realised his hands were steady, no longer shaking.

But Anna was.

Because Mo came back. 'I can't find my shoes.'

'Well, put your slippers on then. And go and get a cereal, in the kitchen.'

'Coco Krispies? Are there Coco Krispies?'

'Yes, they're behind. In the cupboard.'

Mo went away again.

Anna turned back to Hiller. 'Hurry it up. Please hurry.'

But he stood there, not moving. 'She's very important to you, isn't she?'

'Who?'

'Mo . . . I mean, you were serious. When you talked about going away to somewhere quiet and starting all over again.'

'Yes. *Yes*. Come on.'

'Just a minute,' He went towards her. 'You see, I've been thinking . . . about the boy.'

'What about the boy?'

Out of the corner of his eye he saw the grey day. 'If I don't come back tonight . . .'

'. . . You'll come back.'

'But if I don't. I wouldn't want anything to happen too suddenly to him. For it to get out of control.'

122

'Yes, I see that.'

'I mean, I know I can't ask it, but . . .'

'. . . If you're not here,' Anna said, 'I won't let anything like that happen. That's a promise.'

'You mean it?'

'Yes.'

'What I was thinking about was some sort of school for him. A boarding school. Then there'd only be the holidays to think of.'

'Boarding school? But the money?'

'That's the one thing I'll have, after tonight,' Hiller said quietly. 'Whatever happens, the money'll be safe.'

She backed away.

He went after her. 'I told you it was forty thousand, didn't I? I told you it didn't mean anything? Just Monopoly money? . . . And, well, I thought if anything happened to me, half of it should go to the boy. For a school, and after.'

'That's your affair.' She was frightened.

'And the other half I was going to give to you.'

'*Me*?'

'You and Mo. I decided that. It'll help, won't it? You said you wanted to get away and start again?'

'If you think I'm going to touch that money.'

'Look, it's easy. It'll just be there in a Swiss Bank. And I'll find some way for you to pick it up. I promise you that.'

'Will you shut up about it?' She was back against the wall. 'This time tomorrow the whole thing'll be over. And you'll be back here, working out how to spend it.'

'No, I mean it.' Hiller turned away. He didn't want to think about this time tomorrow.

Anna took the children out to the park. She came back at lunchtime, but Hiller couldn't talk to her. The children were always there.

Then at 2.30 Salto and Gort came into the kitchen.

Salto took Hiller over to the window. He spoke softly: 'They're getting your device into the bank at three. And at 'three-thirty they'll ring to say if it's gone all right.'

Hiller nodded. He couldn't speak.

Salto patted his shoulder and went out.

But Gort stayed. He sat down at the table and asked Anna for coffee. And Hiller was surprised by that. Gort, who was working on the team tonight, who'd worked on teams before, was nervous. He needed people around him, and he looked up and saw the boy.

'That's a nice green shirt you got there.'

The boy edged away, remembering the time in the front room.

'And nice green socks too.'

The boy edged further away.

'What you going to be when you grow up then?'

'Green,' the boy said.

Gort held on to his anger. 'Look, I know I smacked your backside. But we can talk, can't we? . . . I got kids too.'

For a moment the boy didn't believe it. But slowly he came back, trying to remember just one good thing about Gort. Then he did. 'Can I see the knife?' he asked.

'The what?'

'Your knife.'

'I haven't got it on me.' Gort was sweating, his black suit suddenly too big for him.

The boy turned away.

'All right.' The knife came out, its blade flashing in the grey afternoon. 'You want to hold it?'

The boy did so, his face pale, impressed. 'What you use it for?'

'Peeling apples.' Hiller felt sorry for Gort then.

'You ever use a gun?' the boy asked.

'No.' Gort hesitated, he saw he was losing the boy's interest. 'I used to pick them up for other people, though, in Geneva. Dead easy to get them in Geneva.' He lowered his voice. 'There was this time I got caught, with this pistol. Dirty great thing. .44 calibre Smith & Wesson Magnum it was, long-barrelled. And straight up, when the Law tested it, that .44 Magnum took the end off the ballistic testing box, went clean through a bench and a concrete wall.'

'.44 what?' the boy asked.

'Smith & Wess . . .'

'. . . Here's your coffee,' Anna said. 'Take it outside.'

At 3.30 Salto came in again. 'It's on,' he said to Hiller. 'They got the device in there. Time to move.'

Hiller had a tightness in his throat. He looked just once at Anna, standing over by the wall with Mo. Then he followed Salto out.

Halfway down the passage he stopped.

'What's up?'

'The boy's in there.' Hiller pointed to the bedroom.

He moved close to Salto. 'I want you to do a couple of things for me,' he said. 'If I don't get back, I want you to make sure Anna gets my money.'

'All of it?' Salto was surprised.

Hiller nodded. 'And if you see trouble coming, I want you to help get the boy away.'

'It's a deal, Hearty.' Salto's dark eyes were suddenly soft.

Hiller went into the bedroom. It was twilit. The boy was by the window playing with a piece of wood and some string. Hiller stroked his hair, feeling the bony skull underneath. He looked out of the window at the street below, the mist that was yellow with exhaust fumes, the blue flicker as the lamps came on. And suddenly he knew he would never see this city again.

'See you,' he said.

'Yeh.'

22

In the town of New Morley the mist was cleaner, the air

sharper as night came down.

And at 7 pm out on the Industrial Estate, a man climbed up a fire escape ladder onto a flat roof. A Link Man. He had two layers of clothes to keep him warm, a tube of Benzedrine tablets to keep him awake. And in a small haversack he had a thermos, binoculars, and a short-wave radio.

He crouched down behind a parapet, got the binoculars out, and focussed them on the gateway across the road. It said ALL NIGHT SECURITY LTD.

At about the same time in the town itself, a second Link Man opened the door of a bed-sitting room. It had one window, overlooking the junction of Queen Street and Orchard Road. The man pulled the chair over to the window and sat down.

A minute or two later, a third Link Man settled himself in the shadow of a ventilator shaft. It was on the roof of Woolworth's, the large new branch in the High Street.

Three-quarters of a mile away at the far end of the High Street was an alley called Harper's Row. It ran alongside the Town Hall.

At 7.15 a man left a green Ford Capri in Harper's Row. The car had fifty pounds of Eversoft plastic explosive in the boot. And the man parked it where he'd been told to, opposite the LEEDS UNITED slogan chalked on the wall.

Because the street-plan of New Morley showed there were underground cables crossing Harper's Row at this point. They were part of the ring-main system that fed the alarms in the town. And they linked the Town Hall with the post offices, jeweller's, department stores, and the banks.

Not that a fifty-pound parcel of Eversoft would reach the cables when it exploded. It couldn't blow a hole through six feet of tarmac, hard core, and soil. But it might just appear to have disturbed the system. And that would

126

help. When the bank alarms started going off.

At 7.20 a man walked through the shadows to the gate of Kramer's Yard. He put a cold chisel through the heavy padlock and hit it with a hammer. Three other men came past him and went on into the Yard. Then he locked the gates again with a new padlock, from the inside.

He joined the others by the workshop door. It took only five minutes to bridge the alarm wires, they were simple. Then the men went inside. They hung blankets over the windows, and started working with pickaxes and shovels. They had more than an hour before the team arrived.

And in that hour the High Street was deserted. New Morley had managed to keep its young people off the streets. The Carlina Café, where the pills changed hands, closed at 6.30. The cinema was showing 'Regal Bingo, Join Today & Play Tomorrow.' And the Youth Centre, with its vaulting horse and boxing gloves donated by Lady Caulfield, was empty.

Nor were there many older people about. In the pubs just a few tired reps sat watching 'Miami Vice'.

Just before 8.30 a Ford 13-tonner went down the High Street. It was painted in yellow and blue, Kramer's colours, and it had KRAMER's on each side. It passed the empty shopping arcade, the store window with VISIT SANTA's CAVE. It passed the winking lights of the Zebra Crossing and the closed Wimpy Bar. Finally it passed the bright frosted windows of the National General Bank.

At the traffic lights it turned left, and left again.

In the back of the 13-tonner the smell was bad. It had come suddenly in the last half hour, when they'd turned off the Motorway. The smell of fear.

There were five of them in the lorry – Hiller, the Guv'nor, the Peterman, the Donkey, and Gort. They wore black trousers and sweaters, and dark cotton gloves. It was only possible to see the glow from their cigarettes.

And then not even that. The lorry stopped, the cigarettes were stubbed out. They were in Kramer's Yard.

The rear doors opened. The men around Hiller dragged out three large bags of padded canvas, with leather grab-handles. They weighed five hundredweight each.

They took them into the workshop. The Guv'nor shut the door and switched on a torch. Its beam found Gort and the Donkey, the steam of their breath. Then it found a new face, a tall man wearing mudstained overalls. He nodded.

Hiller and the Guv'nor followed him past lathes and power-drills, to the corner where the bench had been pulled away. They looked down into the six-foot hole that had been dug. And they saw the gleam of the conduit at the bottom.

The Guv'nor came close to him. 'You all right?'

Hiller nodded.

And he was. Once he was down in the hole, alone with his machines, his hands were quite steady. It was an easy job, as he'd said.

There were three machines. The oscilloscope and simulator were together, in one large metal suitcase. The video-tape unit and the car batteries were in another. Hiller connected them up, and checked that everything was working. Then he went over to the conduit.

He cut his way in. The bank's cables were easy to find. They were separated from the phone-lines, and there were only two of them. The first was the thick multi-core which fed the alarm-systems. He left this one alone. But the second was the co-ax cable which came from the closed-circuit TV.

It was a black quarter-inch cable. At its centre, hidden from view, was the core which carried the TV picture. And around this was the copper braid which guarded it. Because the copper was also carrying a signal, a high-frequency pulse. And if this was interrupted, an alarm would be triggered off.

Hiller reached out for the cable and taped a search-coil

onto it. Then he turned to the oscilloscope. It was a machine with a glass window on which two green lines were being drawn – the upper and the lower trace. Hiller brought the power up to full. And he caught the faint pattern of the pulse – tiny ticks of light appearing on the upper trace.

He moved on to the simulator. With this machine he could generate his own pulse, and show it on the lower trace. He did so. Again there were tiny ticks of light, but in a shifting pattern, bearing no relation to the one above. Hiller worked the controls, slowing the pulse down. The patterns got nearer, until they matched exactly.

He went back to the cable. Very carefully he cut away a small strip of the black insulation and exposed the copper braid. He looped a thin wire round this, and plugged the other end of the wire into the simulator. Now all he had to do was switch over from the bank's pulse to the one he had generated. But at the right time. In between beats.

He waited, watching the ticks of light, nodding his head in time. Then he switched over. It was done.

After that it was simple. The cable between his wire-loop and the bank was now unguarded, he could do what he liked with it. He inserted a probe deep into the inner core, connected up to the video-tape unit, and switched on. Magnetic tape was now recording the TV picture coming from the bank. A wide-angle shot of the ground floor hall. Where nothing moved.

Hiller let the tape run through. Then he switched off. 'TV repair job's done,' he said.

Gort came down into the hole. He passed the two metal suitcases up to the men above, while Hiller paid out the wires. Then both he and Gort climbed out onto the workshop floor.

And they waited, in the dark, the Guv'nor saving torch-light.

At 9.00 pm they heard the distant explosion.

At 9.02 they heard two morse-code dots from the radio

in the Guv'nor's hand.

'Two vans away from the Noddy Depot,' he said. 'Two less for us.'

They heard police sirens, rising and falling in the distance.

And they waited, cigarettes glowing in turn, but faster now.

At 9.04 the Guv'nor switched on the torch again. 'Fags out.'

Hiller bent over the video-tape unit on the floor. He switched it to Transmit. And now the picture that was leaving the bank was the picture of ten minutes ago. Where nothing moved.

At 9.05 Hiller started to make something move.

The device that was large enough to trigger off the VSU alarms.

In his hand he had the toy radio-control handset. He switched it on, pressed the control-stalk forwards, waiting for the bulb to glow.

And in the bank a tubular ashtray started moving.

It was three feet high, of polished chrome, with a heavy rounded base. A base which was a hollow globe, a foot in diameter. And fitted into this were two machines, a radio-control receiver and the mechanism of Hiller's wheeled toy – the tortoise.

Like the tortoise, the ashtray seemed to be searching for brighter light. It came to the dark wainscoting and turned left, it came to a table-leg and turned left again. Then it found what it was looking for – the white line that separated the grey-tiled floor from its black surround.

The ashtray reached the line, went past, and came back as if on elastic, curving round to the left. It homed in on the line again and followed it, wobbling from side to side.

The line changed direction. It came out, following

three sides of a rectangle around a partition. The ashtray overshot the first corner. Whirring angrily, it found the white strip again. And went on. Towards the Overseas & Securities Dept.

In the torchlight Hiller stared at the stopwatch.

The Donkey leaned over him. 'When's it going to happen?'

'Two alarms have to go off,' Hiller told him. 'They're linked in pairs.'

The hand of the stopwatch reached 80 seconds. 'Now,' Hiller said.

He switched off the handset, pulled the control-stalk back to Reverse, and switched on again. Then he re-started the watch.

Around him the men waited.

'When?' the Donkey asked. 'For Christ's sake, when?'

At that moment the Guv'nor's radio signalled. One morse-code dot.

'Just the one Noddy van.' He breathed out slowly. 'We're quids in.'

Hiller was still staring at the watch, frowning as he brought the ashtray back to within a yard of its original position.

At 9.12 there was a second morse dot, higher in pitch.

'Passing Queen Street,' the Guv'nor said. 'Tons of bloody time.'

And Hiller switched off the handset. The ashtray was home.

He switched off the video-tape too. The man watching the TV screen in the Noddy Depot had to see into the bank now. There were going to be people moving in there.

At 9.14, a third, still higher morse dot.

'They're here,' the Guv'nor said. 'Sit down. Fold your arms.'

He switched out the torch.

They heard the sound of brakes from the High Street.

They heard running feet, the jingle of keys, doors opening.

And as they sat there, quite still in the darkness, just the bleep-bleep of the Noddy van's radio . . . on and on.

Then, from over the Yard wall, they heard bolts going back, a door opening. The back door of the bank.

A long silence.

'Nothing,' a man's voice said. 'Nothing.'

'I keep telling you.' Another man's voice. 'There's no windows gone, no locks touched. It's these VSUs. They're up the spout, aren't they?'

The door closed again. The bolts slid home.

Five minutes later they heard the van go away.

And they heard a long morse dash from the radio.

'That's all of them gone,' the Guv'nor said. He switched on the torch.

The Donkey started to get up.

'Sit still.'

And they waited, two more minutes.

Until there was another morse dash from the radio.

'Queen Street,' the Guv'nor said. 'They're going back home.'

The Donkey started dancing, his shadow wild on the wall. 'What'd I tell you, Nob?'

The Peterman looked at him tiredly. He seemed older, smaller without his elevated heels.

'What'd I bleeding tell you?'

'It's all right so far,' the Guv'nor said. 'And that's all.'

At 9.24 Hiller switched the video-tape over to Transmit again.

At 9.25 he switched on the radio-control handset.

And once more the chrome ashtray started moving in the bank.

132

Stopwatch in hand, Hiller timed it. Until it reached the Overseas & Securities Dept., and triggered off the second alarm.

'Now,' he said.

'Now.' Gort was outside the workshop, at the foot of a metal ladder.

The Guv'nor and Peterman were already on the ladder. They went over the wall and dropped into the courtyard on the far side. Then they ran to the back door of the bank.

There were two keyholes. The Peterman had keys. He chose one, tried the lower keyhole. It didn't work.

He bent over the key then, a pen-torch cupped in his hands. He was staring at the marks on the key-blade, where it had been sprayed with silicone.

He thought for a moment, then found another key. It worked. He put a label on it.

The second lock opened without trouble. He labelled this key too.

'One minute,' the Guv'nor said.

Gort reached for the plumber's tool-bag he'd carried over the wall. He got out a heavy compressed air tool. It was fitted with a saw-blade.

The Peterman took it. He slid the blade into the crack between door and door frame, and found the upper bolt. He pressed the trigger. The clatter was huge as the compressed air cartridge fired. And fired again, cutting the lower bolt.

Then they were inside, turning their backs on the light. Gort kept the door ajar while the Peterman worked on the fat steel bolts.

He sawed through the handles, slid the shafts out of their casings on the door, and removed the small stubends from the door frame. Then he took the pieces over to Gort. 'T 38's,' he said.

Gort unrolled a long plastic wallet. It had bolts inside, in separate pockets. He opened the pocket marked T 38.

'Three minutes,' the Guv'nor said.

Gort got out two new bolts. Each was a high-precision

tool. Its handle unscrewed, it had two small electric contacts on its shaft, and further along the shaft – where it would be hidden by the casing – there was a break in the metal.

Gort went with them over to the door. The Peterman was tapping two nails into each bolt-casing, in the worn path where the bolts ran. They were long thin nails, like needles.

He finished, and took the new bolts from Gort. He removed their handles, slipped the shafts into the casings, and screwed the handles on again. Both bolts he left in the locked position. But even so they were short, allowing the door to open.

'Four minutes,' the Guv'nor said.

They cleaned up. Gort swept metal filings into a dustpan. And the Peterman used an Aerosol paint-spray to cover the marks of the saw.

Then they went out, closing the door behind them. Gort knelt over the tool-bag. He got out two long wires, one black, one white. The Peterman took them. Feeling with his hands, he found where the ends of the needle-like nails came through the door. He held the wires against them. Current passed through into a small solenoid inside each bolt. Each one lengthened, clicked home, barring the door. And each could be shortened again, just by reversing the wires.

The Peterman locked the door with the two labelled keys.

'Five minutes,' the Guv'nor said. 'One minute to go.'

They went back over the wall.

And they were sitting in the workshop, arms folded, when the Noddy van arrived.

They heard the bank's front door open in the High Street, heard the bleep-bleep of the radio.

Then the bolts of the back door sliding back. The door opening.

Again a long silence. Then a laugh.

134

'All right, you can laugh.' A younger voice.

'Well, where's the boogy-man then? Where is he? Come on here, boy. Come to daddy.'

The man laughed again and closed the door. The bolts slid home.

At 9.45, the video-tape running, Hiller again worked the handset. And he waited, staring at the watch.

'Now.' The Guv'nor, the Peterman, and Gort went over the wall again.

They got the back door open in 30 seconds, and went on into the bank. They ran down the corridor and came out into the ground floor hall.

Then they stopped. The ashtray was wobbling along the white line, going back home.

'Jesus.' The Peterman shook his head.

He led the way on past the curve of the counter to the employees' gate. It had a simple lock, standard, as had the door to the Manager's Office. The Peterman opened them both, then he held out his hand.

Gort got three huge key-rings from his bag. Each had smaller key-rings on it, labelled in different colours, green, blue, yellow . . .

The Peterman and Guv'nor took one set each. Gort took the third. He went into the Manager's Office.

The other two pushed through the employees' gate. They ran past desks and filing-cabinets, and came to the lift door with its diamond-shaped window.

'Two minutes,' the Guv'nor said. He was standing by the lock on the left of the door.

The Peterman was by the lock on the right.

And in the Manager's Office, Gort was by a third lock, in the wall behind the desk.

It was a three-input lock. There were three different keys, tailor-made, all with the same serial-number. And they all had to be turned at the same time.

The Peterman was kneeling now, close to the right-

135

hand lock. He started sifting through the coloured key-rings, checking serial-numbers. He was careful, and slow.

'Three minutes,' the Guv'nor said.

The Peterman chose the blue ring. He found a key and tried it. It didn't turn. He took it out and examined the silicone coating on the blade.

Then he moved on to the red ring.

In the Manager's Office, Gort was sweating as he watched the clock above the door.

'*Red.*' He heard the Peterman's shout over the office wall. He found the red key-ring and waited.

The Guv'nor waited too, looking at his stopwatch.

'Four minutes,' he said.

'Jesus.' The Peterman snatched a red key from the lock. He stared at it. 'Jesus *Christ*.'

He crouched there, trying to print the key on his mind. Then he put the whole huge key-ring down, shut his eyes, and thought.

It went on a long time.

'Five minutes,' the Guv'nor said. 'We should be finished here.'

Suddenly the Peterman chose a new key-ring. '*Yellow*,' he shouted.

And he started stuffing key after key into the lock.

'Five minutes-fifteen.' The Guv'nor was quite calm.

'*Yellow Six.*'

Gort, in the Manager's Office, found Yellow Six and put it in the lock.

The Guv'nor, to the left of the door, did the same.

They turned the keys.

The lift door hissed open.

They turned the keys back. The door shut.

'Five minutes-thirty,' the Guv'nor said.

Then they were running, keys jangling, for the employees' gate. They went out. The Peterman locked it. Gort locked the Manager's Office.

'Five minutes-forty-five.'

They sprinted for the back door, jerked it open, and

136

shut it behind them. The Peterman locked it.

'Six minutes.'

The Peterman had the black and white wires in his hands. The upper bolt slid home.

'Six minutes-fifteen.'

The lower bolt clicked.

They heard the Noddy van coming as they ran for the wall. Heard it brake as they climbed over. Then they were in the workshop with the others, crouching in the dark.

At 10.05 there were only two of them in the workshop – Hiller and the man in the overalls.

The rest of them were outside, hauling the heavy canvas bags over the wall. The squeal of the pulley seemed loud in the stillness.

Hiller was once again working the handset. For the last time. He finished, and put it down.

The other man was crouching by the video-tape unit. Its spools were turning. 'Now, I just switch off this thing when the Noddy van comes,' he said. 'There's nothing else?'

'That's it.' Hiller turned away. His hands were shaking.

Because by the time the Noddy van came, the man in the overalls would be running things here in the workshop. Hiller would be inside the bank, in the lift shaft.

He waited.

'Time to move,' the man said.

The night was suddenly fresh outside. And quiet, the others had moved on. Hiller stood at the foot of the ladder. There was just the light from the Zebra Crossing in the High Street, yellow and off, yellow and off.

'Get going.' The man was crowding him up the ladder.

He went over the wall. The courtyard on the far side was deserted. In the flashing yellow light he saw the dustbins against the wall. And the door beyond.

It was unlocked. He opened it quietly, and let himself into the bank.

The light dazzled him suddenly. He stood there screwing up his eyes. Then he was able to follow the corridor along to the ground floor hall.

It seemed huge. With its wide empty floor and the hum of air-conditioning, it was like some huge liner steaming through the night.

Then Hiller saw the two other machines, high up in the corner. The TV camera, and the fat black muzzle of the VSU. For a moment he froze. Then he walked on. If he hadn't got it right, it was too late now.

He went past the curve of the counter and came to three men with one of the canvas bags. They were heaving it through the employees' gate. Hiller waited.

And he saw another man. He was carrying a chrome ashtray. It had three small wheels poking out from its underside, and he was taking it away. The bank's original ashtray was back in place.

Hiller turned back to the employees' gate. The men had hauled the bag through now, and he followed them. Over to the lift.

Its door was open. And the lowest of the three buttons – the one marked B – was lit. The lift was down in the basement, the Guv'nor and Peterman standing on its roof, with only their heads and shoulders visible. They were roping the canvas bags onto the main cable. Just the two bags now. The third had held the tools which had got them this far.

They finished, and they signalled Gort and the Donkey in. Then they signalled Hiller.

He climbed down onto the lift roof.

'Put your feet here,' the Guv'nor said. 'Grab onto that cable.'

Hiller did so. And like the other four men, he was leaning in towards the cable, away from the shaft walls.

'Right,' the Guv'nor said.

Out in the hall, a man pressed the button marked G. The lift came smoothly up to its ground floor position. Hiller caught just a glimpse of bright painted walls, then

138

they disappeared below him. He was in a world of cold steel.

The roof of the lift where he was standing had holes cut into it. Thin rays like searchlights came up and found the shiny steel walls of the shaft. On three sides the walls were close, flush with the lift. On the fourth was a narrower shaft where the counterweight came down on its cables, and where there was a ladder. It led up to a service-alcove, forty feet above. And the alcove was opposite a steel door with a diamond-shaped window. The door of the Security Area.

Below them now, and out of sight, the ground floor door hissed shut.

'We're in,' the Guv'nor said. 'Make as much noise as you like. They can't hear us now.'

It was 10.20 when the Noddy Men came in through the main doors. There were four of them, with helmets, nightsticks, and with smoke-masks hanging from their necks. The masks should have been clipped in place, but the men had made the same journey three times already tonight, and they were moving slowly.

Except for the young man. His face was pale inside his helmet, and scared. He marched away, putting his boots down hard as he checked the windows.

The others sat down and took off their helmets. The Sergeant was sweating under his grey cropped hair.

The young man came back. 'Nothing,' he said.

'Get away.' The Sergeant didn't like him. 'Look, seeing as how you're so bloody keen, you can take the first watch.'

He led the young man over to the Manager's Office, unlocked it, and then unlocked the control-panel inside on the wall. There was a small TV screen. The Sergeant switched it on. It showed a bare steel passage.

'That's inside the Security Area,' he said. 'The passage into the Strong Room. Just you stay watching that.'

'What'm I supposed to be looking for, Sarge?'

'You'll see two, no three men, won't you?' the Sergeant said tiredly. 'Dark, ugly-looking buggers with Burglar written on their backs. And they'll have this machine on wheels, like the sort they have in hospitals.'

He went out of the office and unlocked the employees' gate.

In the lift shaft, Hiller was climbing the metal ladder. Climbing it slowly, afraid, his breath coming in clouds of steam. It was cold in the shaft. The central heating didn't come this far.

He reached the service-alcove. It was a hollow steel box, eight feet by eight, let into the side of the shaft. It had lifting gear, a workbench, and power points. But Hiller wasn't looking at these. He was looking at the black quarter-inch cable, the second TV line. It came up to the level of the alcove, then went across the shaft to the Security Area on the far side. The door had two buttons, Secure and Admit. And through the diamond-shaped window, Hiller could see the passage that led to the Strong Room.

The Guv'nor and the Donkey were using the lifting gear to haul up the first of the canvas bags. They swung it into the alcove, then looked back down the shaft.

Forty feet below on the lift roof, Gort unroped the second bag from the main cable. It slipped away from him, fell against the shaft wall. He went after it.

Outside in the ground floor hall, the Sergeant idly pressed the lift-button marked S.

Hiller heard the huge click of the machinery, and then the shriek. The Guv'nor grabbed them back against the wall as the lift came up. Gort's head came first, thrown back, screaming. Then he was above them as the lift stopped at the Security Area.

Another click, and it came down again. It left a dull smear, a foot wide, all the way down the steel shaft wall.

The screams got louder.

Out in the hall, the Sergeant heard nothing. He turned away as the lift reached the ground floor. 'Anyone remember to bring that coffee?'

The Guv'nor went fast down the ladder, hand over hand.

Gort screamed without stopping. His body was lodged crookedly against the edge of the lift, one leg between it and the shaft wall. The Guv'nor blocked out half his mind, and hauled the leg out. It was thin and pulped. The Guv'nor laid it down. Then he unblocked more of his mind. He saw the blood that was pumping out of the artery.

He peeled off his sweater and wrapped it round the leg. He peeled off his shirt and trousers and did the same. Then he saw it wasn't going to be enough.

'Sling us an empty bag down here,' he shouted. 'Quick.'

He heard them unloading the bag far above, the clink of metal. And he waited, his face expressionless in the tiny shafts of light. He didn't look at Gort's face.

Then he heard the sound of the lifting gear.

'Don't lower it. *Sling* the fugging thing down.'

He shielded his head with his arms. The heavy sack fell on him, knocking him down. He got up, folded it into three thicknesses, and wrapped it round the stump of the leg.

Still he didn't look at Gort's face. Because he wasn't thinking about Gort, he hadn't thought about him once. He was thinking about the blood, how it would seep through the holes in the roof to the lift below. How it would be seen by anyone looking in through the window. To him Gort was already dead.

'Let's have that rope now,' he shouted. 'We'll haul it up.'

Hiller had two more metal suitcases open. One with an oscilloscope and a simulator. The other with a video-tape unit and batteries. He turned towards the black quarter-inch cable, the second TV line. Stared at it.

Behind him in the alcove Gort was moaning. Air whistled into his mouth and whistled out again.

Hiller reached out for the cable with a search-coil. His hands shook as he taped it on.

'Get moving.' The Guv'nor was bare-legged, shivering. He had the Donkey's huge sweater on. His face and hands were streaked with blood.

Hiller worked the oscilloscope. He brought the power up. And he saw the pattern of the high-frequency pulse, the ticks of light on the upper trace.

He moved on to the simulator, and generated his own pulse on the lower trace. But its pattern was wild. His hand, shaking on the control, could make no sense of it.

He looked round. He meant to look at the Guv'nor, but he saw Gort. His face slab-white, blue round the mouth where the air whistled in. And his leg trussed up, dark like a ham.

'You want me to ring for a fugging doctor?' the Guv'nor shouted. 'Is that what you want?'

Hiller turned back to the simulator. He fought his hand on the control, made it get the pattern near to the one on the upper trace.

Near enough. He left it.

Then he felt the Guv'nor's breath. 'Get that right.'

Hiller did so. He matched the two patterns exactly.

He went back to the cable. He had a precision-tool, a cable-stripper with a blade that could be set in thous. It should have been easy to lay bare the copper braid without setting off the alarm. Should have.

But Gort's moans were running together, making words:

'. . . . Smith & Wesson Magnum . . .'

It was this afternoon, when he'd talked to the boy in the flat.

'. . . .44 calibre, straight up . . .'

Hiller took a deep breath. He braced his arm against the wall, and made the cuts.

The copper braid gleamed. It was unharmed.

He looped a wire round it, and plugged it into the simulator.

Now he had to switch over from the bank's pulse to his own. At the right time. Between beats.

His hands went to the two knobs. He stared at the traces.

'. . . .44 Magnum. Took the end off the ballistic . . .'

Hiller sagged away from the machine. If it had been just the one knob, he might have managed. But two. Both hands.

'. . . Clean through a bench and a concrete . . .'

There was a squeal. Hiller swung round.

The Guv'nor had stuck a square of Band-Aid over Gort's mouth. 'Get on with it,' he said.

Hiller reached for the knobs again. But it was no good. There was a wet sucking noise behind him. Gort was choking.

And Hiller remembered something else Gort had said this afternoon: 'I got kids too.'

He backed away from the machine and shook his head.

The Guv'nor didn't look at him, or Gort, he was looking in between. And there was some animal thing about him which made him read the situation. Made it just a simple choice.

He reached out and pinched Gort's nose. Hard. Holding him down.

Gort kicked. And with each kick, the canvas round his leg got darker.

'Do it,' the Guv'nor said.

Hiller couldn't move.

'Do it *quick*.'

Hiller's head was in his hands. He took a deep breath, held himself quite still. Then he turned back to the machine and stared at the ticks of light. He switched over.

The Guv'nor let go of Gort's nose. 'Is it all right?'

Hiller nodded.

'Finish it,' the Guv'nor said.

Hiller put the probe into the core of the cable, and plugged it into the video unit. He recorded the TV picture coming from the Security Area. Then he switched the tape over to Transmit.

'It's done.'

He was trapped then against the side of the alcove, while the others went to work. They laid a steel ladder across the shaft. The Peterman went over and pressed the Admit button. The door opened. The Donkey went over too. He had a rope attached to the cutting-gear – the thermic lance. It was fitted with wheels that gripped the rails of the ladder. And he hauled it over. The Guv'nor followed.

It was only then that Hiller could get to Gort.

And Gort was dead.

His face was strangely thin and messy, collapsed round the strip of Band-Aid, and there was mucus from his nose. Hiller looked across at the men in the steel-lined corridor, the cleanness of it, not a speck of dust. And he didn't understand.

He turned to the black TV cable. He didn't understand that either. What Gort's death had meant.

Until he saw the part that was wrong.

The last part of the job. The easy part.

The probe was in crookedly, missing the central core, not intercepting the TV picture at all.

Down in the Manager's Office, the young man looked up from his war book. He saw the monitor screen.

'Sarge.' He ran from the office.

23

Head down, the Guv'nor sprinted back down the passage and crossed the shaft. He helped the Donkey with the thermic lance. The Peterman came last, closing the door.

And they waited.

The Sergeant came slowly into the Manager's Office. He'd been asleep. He looked at the TV screen. It showed just an empty steel-lined passage.

'What was it you saw again?'

'There were three of them,' the young man said.

The Sergeant worked the controls under the screen. When the picture refirmed, it again showed just an empty passage.

'Once more.' He turned back to the young man.

'What, Sarge?'

'Tell me just once more.'

'Three dark men.' The boy looked away. 'With this machine like you see in hospitals.'

The Sergeant saw the war book on the desk. 'Fuggoff,' he said.

And he went out.

The Guv'nor had a small WD transmitter. He tapped out three call-signs, on different frequencies.

The Link Men answered. Each with a long dash.

The Guv'nor waited. He tried in ten minutes, he tried in twenty minutes. Each time he got the same reply. All Clear.

He looked at the Peterman. The Peterman nodded.

Hiller crouched back against the wall.

But the Guv'nor just looked at him, his veins standing out as he held onto his anger. 'You can get that right now, can't you?' was all he said.

Hiller went back to the TV cable. It took him five minutes.

The others fitted the ladder across the shaft and went back into the Security Area.

Then the Guv'nor turned round to Hiller. 'You don't want to stay there?' He pointed at Gort's body. 'With that?'

The Strong Room door filled the end of the passage. There

was just a handle with a small name-plate – Sanger's. Nothing else.

Hiller stared at the size of it, the light bouncing off the polished steel. He tried not to think of Gort any more. He tried to think only of the mechanism inside the door.

The time-lock. It operated steel pistons, six inches thick, which fitted into the door frame. There were sixteen of them, four on each side. And the door itself was nine inches thick.

The Peterman knelt in front of it. With a pair of dividers he drew a circle, a yard in diameter. He pulled on a gas-mask with tinted lenses. Then he turned to the thermic lance.

It was 11.31.

It was 3.30 am by Hiller's watch. The passage had disappeared, the Strong Room door had disappeared, in thick white smoke. As solid as cotton wool.

Through his gas-mask, Hiller could only see the Peterman, the small crab of a man. He was crouching over a knife-point of brilliant white. And he'd been there, his arms steady, for four solid hours. Five minutes break every hour.

Hiller couldn't hear the roar any longer. It had gone through him. He could only see the three-quarter circle the Peterman had cut in the door. The last foot of it was red hot, the last six inches white. The lance cut through the steel at a rate of one inch every three minutes.

Tiredly, Hiller made another calculation. The passage was 40 ft long, 8 ft high, 8 ft wide. 2,560 cu ft of air. No more, because the lift door had been closed, and the air-conditioning vents blocked. . . . 2,560 cu ft of dirty air. There was a real risk of the thermic lance blowing back. And if that happened, maybe two out of the four of them would still be alive. But they wouldn't be able to crawl back to the lift.

Not that it mattered. Nothing mattered any more.

It was 6.00 am. The Peterman had now worked for six hours, with five minutes off every hour. Hiller could hardly see his head.

Or the white-hot line which joined up with the curve of the first cut.

With a huge crash, the circle of steel fell in through the door.

The Peterman switched off. But he didn't let go, of himself, or the thermic lance.

The Guv'nor appeared in the smoke. He laid a pad of asbestos over the patch of white hot steel.

Stiff, bent double, the Peterman went through the hole, dragging the cables with him. He was in a passage. There were heavily barred doors. The Peterman switched on the lance again and cut through the two locks the Guv'nor showed him. He had to be shown. He was strange, his body set in the one position.

Then he sat down, slowly, feeling his way. He took off his mask. The air was clean and sweet around him. There was just a fat tube of white smoke coming through the hole in the door.

And through those other doors he'd opened – the barred doors – there were metal cases. Securi-Cor, Security Express, All Night Security Ltd. Pay-rolls and takings.

£12,875,000 in cash.

24

The boy got out of bed in Salto's flat. He saw that Mo was asleep in the other bed, and he wondered about that as he went to the bathroom.

Then he stopped in the passage. The door of the next

room was ajar, he could hear voices – Anna's, and a woman's voice he didn't know.

'How much longer are you going to be tied up here then?' the woman asked.

'Not long,' Anna said. 'I'm nearly there now. I know I can get half, but there's more. Maybe I can get the whole thing.'

'You always said there was money here, didn't you?'

'That's right.'

The boy didn't know what they were talking about. But he knew the tone of voice. It reminded him of the mornings years ago when it had all been simple, when his parents had talked softly in their room across the landing. It warmed him. And he stood there for a moment, listening.

'But *twenty*? How did you get him to give you twenty grand?' the woman asked. 'You must have really got through to him.'

'No,' Anna said, 'he wouldn't have gone for anything like that. It was sort of through the kids. I just made out we could all get on. He's the sort who wants to believe that. He's been kicked around by women before, and he'll get kicked around again.'

'So what happens now?'

'Well, it can only go two ways, can't it?' Anna said. 'Either he comes back from the bank all in one piece, the kid goes off with him, and I get half the money . . . Or else he doesn't come back, he gets put inside, and I get all the money.'

'What about the kid then?'

'You know how it is with me and kids,' Anna said slowly. 'I mean, you know if anyone does.'

The woman gave a strange laugh.

The boy frowned. He didn't understand the laugh. But he knew they were talking about him now. He went closer to the door.

'I'm not looking after him a day longer than I have to,' Anna said. 'It'll just have to be that sick little joke called Care, won't it? Where I was dragged up . . . Christ, I hope it's changed in fifteen years.'

'It must have.'

'Well, he's not my problem, is he? Anyone with half a mind. . . I mean, it was his mother who ran off. She didn't want to have anything to do with him.'

Out in the passage the boy turned his face to the wall. He gave a low cry.

There were footsteps suddenly. Anna came round the door and grabbed him, grabbed him hard. There was a moment's real fear on her face.

'How long've you been there?'

He didn't answer.

'How *long*?'

'Only a sec. I . . .' He pointed round at the bathroom.

'But you heard?'

'No,' the boy lied.

There was the sound of the other woman stirring inside the room. 'He can't have understood anything, can he?' she called out. 'Well, can he?'

'I don't know.' Anna squatted down, her face close to the boy's. She was frowning now, working it out.

'Your da . . . Your stepfather went out tonight,' she said. 'You're all on your own, aren't you?'

He stared at her, afraid. And the thing that made him afraid was that she wasn't trying to frighten him – he knew that. She was just going through it as she saw it, step by step.

'You see, he might come back in the morning.' She pulled him closer. 'Or he might come back . . . in a few days' time.'

He nodded.

'But when he does come back . . . I don't want you to tell him anything about tonight.'

He nodded again.

She bit her lip. She was searching for a way to keep him quiet. She knew there was a way.

And then she saw it.

Because suddenly he was pulling back, turning his head

away. From her legs which were bare under her overcoat, from her hair which was stuck to her forehead. From the smell of lick.

'You see why we can't tell him anything, don't you?' she asked.

He flushed. He saw some of it.

But she made him see more. With one hand she made an unambiguous gesture on the front of her body.

'You do see?'

'Fixing up,' he said softly.

'What?'

'Fixing . . . up.'

She looked down at him a moment. Then she reached out deliberately and opened the door.

He saw the woman on the bed, pulling the sheets around her.

'But like *that*?' The blush spread down his neck.

'Just like that,' Anna said. 'And that's why we can't say anything about it.'

There was something oddly similar then about their two heads. Both hard, quite still, staring at one another.

'All right then?' It was a bargain struck on her side.

And on his, the sudden lurch from innocence to knowing, the burden.

25

It was nearly 7 am. The lift was crowded with men and sacks. It went smoothly down from the Security Area. And Hiller, still in his gasmask, was afraid.

He was sure now they'd been seen on the closed circuit TV. Sure there'd be people waiting out in the ground floor hall.

And the Guv'nor was taking risks. By letting them all go

down in the lift. Instead of climbing down the shaft and cutting their way through the lift-roof. There hadn't been time.

They reached the diamond-shaped window of the ground floor. The door hissed open. The Guv'nor and Donkey slipped out. It was quiet. They wore gasmasks. They each had a CS gas grenade.

Hiller waited. It was too quiet. The soft footsteps went away. Then he heard the grenades rolling on the tiled floor. Heard the gasps. The single shout. Before the silence.

The two masked men came back. The Guv'nor picked up one money-sack, the Peterman took the second, Hiller the third. The Donkey put the last sack over his shoulder. It was heavy and stiff. Gort.

They ran past the wreaths of CS gas, the four black-uniformed men gasping, trying to crawl.

They got the main doors open. It was grey outside. There were two Jaguars by the kerb.

They reached the first one. They threw the sacks into it and slammed the doors. The engine roared. Wheels spinning, the car went away.

The street was deserted. Except for the one workman, watching. He had a thermos and a sandwich tin. He came towards them.

They ran for the second car. Hiller got in, the Peterman got in. But the Donkey spun round towards the man with the thermos. Hiller saw the baseball bat, saw the Donkey's shoulders, his huge anger.

The Guv'nor got to him first. He grabbed the bat, swung the Donkey away. Then he was after the man, kicking him, and again, low down. The man fell. His thermos smashed.

They were all in the car, the engine bellowing, the Guv'nor ripping off his mask and banging his fist down, locking the doors.

Only the Stoppo was small and calm. He was low down in his fitted seat, with strips of foam rubber between him

151

and the door. He wore a racing helmet.

The crackle of voices came from inside it. A radio link.

The Stoppo hit the brakes suddenly. Hiller, the Guv'nor were jerked forward around his shoulders. The Stoppo grunted, taut against his harness. He twitched the wheel. The car slid.

There were screams, heads smacking on the windows as the car spun round, facing the way it had come. Then it went back. Past the man with the smashed thermos.

Again the crackle of voices from the racing-helmet. The Stoppo hesitated, lifted his foot.

The voices came once again.

The Stoppo braked, reversed, looking back.

'What in *hell*?' the Guv'nor shouted.

The car stopped.

VISIT SANTA'S CAVE.

Hiller didn't believe it. They mounted the pavement, roared down the narrow arcade. The lit windows, radiograms, carpets, flicked past.

Then he saw the metal post at the far end. NO CYCLING.

The Stoppo dabbed at the brakes, flicked the wheel. The car slid, four wheels, sideways. The back end took the metal post, buckled it. Hiller was thrown against the doorframe as the rear of the car came back, smacked into dustbins, the front of a shop, and came back again.

Then they were out. One tyre gone, but they were out by the carpark.

The tyre didn't seem to bother the Stoppo. He took the needle into the red, through second and third gears.

Hiller didn't see any more. The window by him was frosted, smashed. He heard only the crackle of voices from the Stoppo's helmet. And the man himself swearing as he braked, changed down, barrelled the power onto the road.

Then they slowed. There were lock-up garages, one with its door open. The Stoppo drove straight in and hit the wall at the far end.

Shaking, Hiller couldn't move. The Guv'nor pulled him out. The others were out too. They were fighting to get out of the narrow space.

The Guv'nor blocked their way. 'Don't leave a thing. Not a blind *thing.*'

He made them check the inside of the car. Then he led them out of the garage and pulled its door shut.

There was the arch of a motorway, the drone of cars above them. The Guv'nor hauled Hiller along in its shadow. They went over a wall. They came to an identical row of garages on the far side.

A stolen McAlpine van was there, a driver behind the wheel. They got in. There was a pile of gumboots and McAlpine jackets. The others pulled them on. Hiller did the same.

They went up on the motorway, following the signs for London. The Guv'nor got the fags out.

'It looks like we copped the bastard, didn't we?' He leaned back, breathing out smoke.

Then he saw the morning paper.

SURREY PC DIES IN IRA BLAST.

26

'Turn the fugging thing round. Get *off* the motorway.'

'What d'you mean?' The driver turned.

'Get the hell away from London. Make for the A 30.'

The Guv'nor hunched forward on his seat. All the tension returned. He didn't speak for a long time.

'Stop at the next phone box,' he said then.

The driver did so.

'Now you get hold of Monty,' the Guv'nor told him. 'You don't try to get hold of *anyone* else, just Monty. And you tell him the whole thing's been shot to hell.'

The man nodded. He was frightened.

'You tell him we're going to use that route I had put by. You tell him that van *has* to be waiting for us with the clothes inside. You got that?'

'Okay.'

'And one more thing. You get to somewhere quiet and you keeep your head down. That's for your own good.'

The man got out quickly and walked away. The Guv'nor took over the wheel.

For Hiller the rest of the day was a blur between sleeping and waking. There was the multi-storey carpark in South-ampton where they changed to the second van, changed into dark business suits, and shaved. There was the Machine Tools Show in Exeter where they walked all afternoon with the crowds. And there was the long slow drive out of the city in the dark, the chain of headlights stretching out ahead and behind.

Then they turned away from the main road and the lights. They went down a dark steep hill to the sea.

It was a bleak Victorian terrace on the edge of a town. There were just the houses, and facing them across the road, a railway line, and the beach below. The wind boomed in from the huge black sea, swinging the signs in the doorways, Sea-View, Rest-A-While. They were boarding houses, sad, with just a few windows lit. And at the far end of the terrace, none. The windows were shut-tered there, waiting for summer.

The Guv'nor drove to the end of the terrace. He drove on past a stretch of waste land and came to some sheds. He switched out his lights and waited. Then he parked in one of the sheds, and felt in his pocket for a key.

The torchlight showed a long room with damp patches on the ceiling. It was cold, Hilller and the other four men sat wrapped in blankets. And behind them on the wall a notice said the First Floor Bathroom was Shared Weds and Sats Under Agreement.

The Guv'nor switched on the radio. He kept it low.

'. . . Both IRA and Protestant Extremists have denied responsibility for last night's explosion in New Morley.

And it's now known that the blast was connected with the robbery at the National General Bank. A police spokesman claimed that the constable first noticed the car at 7.30 pm. It was badly parked, with one wheel obstructing the pavement . . .'

'Jesus,' the Guv'nor shouted.

'. . . At 8.58 the constable was returning on his beat. He was just approaching the car when it exploded . . .'

'Jesus *Christ*.'

'. . . The blast damaged underground cables, causing the false alarms . . .'

'That's not how it was,' the Peterman said.

'. . . The thieves got away with over £2,000,000 in cash . . .'

'That's not how it was at all. Not the money, not anything.'

'No,' the Guv'nor said. 'They're playing it down.'

He switched off the radio. There was just the battering of the wind.

'You know who it is then?' He turned to the Peterman.

'The Yard.'

'That git Freeman,' The Guv'nor nodded. 'And Freeman gets names.'

'Not our names, for Christ's sake. We're in good all over London.'

'With a dead copper on his hands, he'll get names.'

All that night Hiller lay awake, listening to the house shaking as the trains came by, listening to the voices arguing all round him. And he knew it was bad.

But he didn't know how bad until just before dawn.

Because Anna arrived, with Mo and the boy.

She was exhausted, she'd been up all night. And she looked around at the shadows, the peeling wallpaper, not believing any of it.

'That bloody kid of yours,' she said.

'What are you talking about?'

'They said he had to be got away. They said he knew

155

things.'

'What things? What could he know?'

She shook her head.

'And where's Salto?'

'He's coming.'

'When?'

'How do I know?' Her voice rose. 'How do I know what I'm doing here? What Mo's doing here? Or *any* bloody thing?'

Mo was hidden, pressed into the folds of her coat.

And the boy, some way away, seemed very small and alone. Suddenly he ran at Hiller and grabbed his knees.

Hiller was amazed.

But he wasn't prepared for what came next. The strange mask-like smile on the boy's face. The falseness of it.

Later they were all in the room with the radio.

'. . . Announced tougher penalties for aiding and abetting guerillas,' the news-reader said. 'And now, the weather . . .'

The Guv'nor switched off.

'It's a good news today.' The boy touched Hiller's arm. Again there was that cloying smile.

'Quiet,' Hiller said.

But he went on: 'Aiding and abetting gorillas. The news is quite good this morning.'

There was silence in the room. Then the Donkey turned.

'Come over here.'

The boy sat quite still.

'Over *here*.'

Anna moved. She picked up both children and pushed them out of the door.

But the Donkey got to her before she could follow. He grabbed her shoulder. Then the anger in him changed. His hands moved on down her body.

She slammed the door into him. He was leaning for-

156

ward, there was blood. She twisted free and ran after the children.

Hiller caught up with them on the top landing. They went through the first door they came to. Anna locked it. Then she threw the boy on the bed. His head hit the rail.

'That's enough,' Hiller said.

But she turned away, pressing herself against the door, listening.

Hiller went towards her. 'Look, I know it's not easy, but there's no need . . .'

'. . . No *need*?' She swung round. 'You don't know any bloody thing, do you?'

'What d'you mean?'

'In the car last night.'

'What about the car?'

'There was this rolled up blanket. There were guns.'

'Guns?' His mouth opened. 'But they never used guns before. All the time I . . .'

'. . . Christ help us. Don't you see? The sort of bird they're handing out nowadays.'

'The sort of what?' Hiller didn't recognise her any more. Not her anger, the words she used, anything.

'Listen,' she shouted. 'They're putting people inside for thirty or forty *years*.'

It took him a moment to understand.

'That's it.' She nodded. 'And what you got to realise is that this lot down here . . . they just don't care any more.'

She turned then and pointed at the bed: 'So you just keep that bloody kid of yours quiet. You keep his mouth tight shut until Salto gets here. Though Christ knows what he's going to do about it now.'

Dazed, Hiller took the boy away through a door. There was a hardboard partition dividing the room in two. And on the other side were a bed, a table, and chairs. They were covered in plaster. A deep crack ran across the ceiling to the window.

More plaster fell. The window-frame shook as a train came past, slowing for the station in the town.

27

Salto came on the midday train. It took him half an hour to walk from the station. And he came in the back way, through the garden.

'It's all right,' he said.

Nobody spoke.

'Monty fixed it. It's all right.' There was mist on Salto's suede coat, on his airline briefcase. And faced by the five exhausted men in the hall, he was suddenly young and powerful.

'How d'you mean, all right?' the Guv'nor asked.

'Well, for a start, the money got through. So . . .'

'. . . For Christ's sake.'

'I was trying to tell you,' Salto said. 'Monty reckons he can get you away this afternoon.'

'How?'

'He got onto a French firm. He had to do that. Nobody's helping over here.'

'Yes,' the Guv'nor said. 'I see that.'

'There's a Piper Saratoga, twin-engined job,' Salto went on. 'It got down this morning along the coast here. It'll take off again at three. He won't leave it any later.'

'He? Who is he?'

'Canadian flyer. He's working in Europe.'

'Tight-mouthed?'

Salto nodded. 'And pricey.'

'I don't care about that,' the Guv'nor said. 'You did good.'

He went away through the shadows. He put his head back against the wall and he breathed out.

'What time do we leave here?' he asked then.

'Two, at the latest,' Salto said. 'That'll give us enough time.'

'And what's the Law situation like?'

'It's good round here. They're all over London, the air-port, and the Channel ports. But not much this way.'

'So we can use the van?'

'I reckon so. Maybe I can drive with the girl and the two kids up front. And maybe you four can be in the back, under a rug.'

'You *four*?' Hiller spoke for the first time.

Salto looked round. 'You won't be going,' he said. 'Your kid goes. But you stay here.'

He came over to where Hiller stood by the stairs. 'You're the biggest trouble we've got right now,' he said quietly.

'Me?'

'That's right. They heard about the Print-Out thing.'

'They *what*?'

Salto spread his hands. 'The word is this, dear Heart. . . It seems the Law never could understand how we got into the bank. So they talked to Sanger's, who put the locks on the place, and they talked to ILR's. They checked on everyone who'd left in the past year.'

Hiller turned away. He leant on the banisters.

'And what they came up with at ILR's was the Com-missionaire. Because it seems he remembers you going back there that day. And what's more he remembers you still had your Security Pass with you. There was a hell of a fuss . . . They found out you printed the tape. Then they checked on every damn Computer Bureau in the country until they came up with the right bit of paper. And then . . . Then they checked with your wife. They found out you had the kid.'

Hiller stared at the banister rail, the white paint, and where it had been rubbed brown at the turn.

'So you see how it is, dear Heart? For the next six months, you walk down any street in Europe with that kid, and you get done.'

He stared through the banisters at the floor beyond, the rotting lino, the damp.

Then there were shoes coming over the lino. The

Guv'nor's.

'You get done, and we *all* get done,' he shouted. 'Because there's this guy called Chief Superintendent Freeman. And he's just waiting for that kid. Waiting to send out for a gallon of ice cream.'

'Hold on a moment,' Salto cut in. 'Look, I said six months, didn't I, Heart? It'll only be six months, the time you're away from the boy.'

'What d'you mean?'

'Well, there's a way of doing these things. It has to be done right,' Salto said. 'There's the safe kip we've got to find for you. There's the plastic surgery, the hair transplant, the health farm bit to get your weight down . . . And then there's your papers, they have to go way back. That's what takes the time.'

'But all that?' Hiller's throat was dry suddenly. 'You're going to do all that for me?'

'Listen,' The Guv'nor pushed his way between them, 'it's quite simple. You were with us inside the bank, you did a good job for us. So now we see you get clear and get paid. I've always been strong on things like that . . . That is, so long as you play it clever.' He grabbed Hiller's collar. 'There isn't going to be any bother when that kid leaves here. He just goes away.'

Hiller turned his head. Behind the Guv'nor he saw the others moving in. He saw the way their coats sagged. The guns. And he saw their eyes.

'All right.' He nodded.

'That's okay then.' The Guv'nor let him go.

'But . . .' Hiller backed away '. . . I mean, six months? Who's going to look after the boy all that time?'

The Guv'nor looked past him, up the stairs. 'There's her, isn't there? The way I heard it, you were quite close.'

'I don't know,' Hiller said. 'I'm not sure any more.'

'Well, I'd say you had to fix something up,' the Guv'nor said. 'I'd say it was important.'

Hiller turned away. His feet got slower and slower as he climbed to the room where Anna was . . . Six months . . .

All at once he knew she wasn't going to do it, wasn't going to have anything to do with them. She was frightened. *That bloody kid.*

She opened the door no more than a crack, her face grey and drawn. It made no difference when she saw it was him. He went into the room. The boy was sitting at one end of the bed, Mo at the other, both quite still. He didn't know where to begin.

'Lock the door,' Anna said.

'There's no need.'

'*Lock* it.'

'It's all right,' Hiller told her. 'Salto's here. He's going to get you away this afternoon.'

She didn't believe him. She went back to the bed, keeping herself between him and Mo, shielding her.

'There's a plane,' Hiller said. 'It landed this morning, along the coast.'

'No,' she said. 'Salto couldn't fix anything like that.'

'It's not Salto. He's come from another man. Someone called Monty.'

The name didn't mean anything to her.

'You leave here in just over an hour, at two o'clock,' Hiller said. 'You go along the coast in the van. The plane leaves at three.'

He went towards her. Mo came into view, pulling at her sleeve. 'The chocklit, mummy. You said there was some chocklit.'

'Not now.' Anna shook her head. 'It's for later.'

'For on the plane,' Hiller said.

Her fingers were stiff, pressed against her mouth. 'No. It couldn't be that simple.'

'But it's true,' Hiller shouted. 'The plane's come from France. It belongs to some French people. There's a Canadian pilot . . . Go down and ask Salto.'

'Canadian . . . . ?' She turned towards him.

'What?'

'Canadian pilot? Nobody could make that up.'

'No.'

Suddenly she believed him. Her face, her hands softened, and she lay back on the bed. 'Thank Christ.'

'Chocklit, mummy. Chocklit.' Mo bounced on her.

'Yes,' Anna said. She got the bar from her pocket and broke it in four pieces. 'Hand it round. Go on.'

Hiller took a piece and ate it. Then he wiped his hands, they were sweating. 'There's just one thing,' he said.

'What's that?' She wasn't really listening.

'You remember once, you said you'd help out with the boy?'

'Yes.'

'Well, would you look after him, on the plane? And . . . and afterwards for a while?'

'I don't see why not.'

Then she turned. She saw how tense he was.

'Only . . . I won't be coming,' Hiller said.

She stared at him.

'I've got to stay here for a while.'

'Stay?'

'In England. Is that going to make any difference?'

'No difference,' she said slowly. 'No difference at all.'

'You're sure about that? You'll still look after the boy?'

'Yes.'

'Look,' he bent close to her. 'I have to tell you this. I've got to change my face, get a new hairstyle. There's been trouble . . . Not that any of it'll come back on you,' he added quickly. 'You'll be miles away. And no-one's going to come looking for the boy. There hasn't been a photo of him, not for years.'

'It's all right,' she said.

'And when I say a while,' he hesitated, 'it'll be six months. They said six months before I could pick him up. I know it's a lot to ask. I know that.'

'Six months isn't long.' She was quite calm. He was amazed at her calmness.

'But are you sure?' he asked again. 'I mean, you'll take care of him?'

She nodded. 'I said I'd help out, didn't I?'

'And I said I'd . . .' he stood up and led her away from the children. '. . . There's the money part.'

She didn't say anything.

'It's easy, I can get Salto to arrange it.' He lowered his voice. 'He'll tell you which bank in Switzerland. He'll tell you the number of the account, and the name to sign. That's all you'll have to know.'

Still she didn't say anything.

'So take half, like I promised you. Or take more than half. I don't care, just as long as you leave me a little to . . .'

He stopped. He couldn't work out what there was on her face. Disgust?

Then it was gone. And he stood there, trying to understand: 'Look, I know you didn't want to have anything to do with it. But you'll have to use the money now. If you're going to look after the boy.'

'Yes,' she said, 'I suppose so.'

'Suppose so?' He was excited suddenly. 'By tea-time you'll be out of the country. What will you do? Where will you go?'

'I don't know.' Slowly she turned to the little girl. 'What d'you reckon? Where shall we go and live?'

'Seaside,' Mo said.

'All right. Somewhere in the sun.' Anna thought for a moment. 'What about . . . I know, what about Palma? I was there once. We could get a flat overlooking the sea . . . There's the cathedral, the harbour, and all the yachts. There's an English school too. You could go off every morning with . . .'

She turned. The boy had gone through the partition door.

'I'll talk to him,' Hiller said.

He went through to the other room. And he no longer saw the greyness of it, the fallen plaster. There was a great brightness coming from the window, a very white light. The wind had gone, there was a mist far out over the sea, and the water was smooth, the colour of metal.

And there was the boy too, crouching by the window,

his face small and creased. There was something about him, something strangely old.

28

'What's the time?'

'Again?' Hiller looked at his watch. 'Three minutes since you asked me the last time.'

'Three minutes?'

'Yes.' And in that time he'd told the boy about the flat in Palma, the harbour and the yachts. And all the while the boy had kept his back turned, avoiding Hiller's hand as it reached out for him.

'But I'll be there in six months. It'll be all right, won't it?' Hiller asked now. 'I mean, it was all right before, in that other flat?'

He didn't answer.

'Well, wasn't it?'

The boy kept quite still. 'What's the time?' he asked again.

'Half past.'

'Half an hour to go.' It was no more than a whisper.

'Yes. Is there anything you want?'

There was a long pause.

'Tell me a story,' the boy said then.

'Story?' Hiller frowned. 'I thought you didn't like my stories any more.'

'Go on.'

'Well. What one d'you want to hear?'

'Our one.'

'You mean . . . The Continuing Saga of Sod's Law?' The words seemed strange and faraway.

'That's it.'

164

'But it's all over. Finished.'

'Go on.'

'I don't know.' Hiller sat down on the bed. 'I can't tell it if you don't look at me.'

But the boy still didn't turn from the window. There seemed to be a huge amount of white sky around him. He seemed to be holding onto the window-sill as though he could fly up into it.

'Tell me about the Good Time,' he said.

'What Good Time?'

'When the Princess wore a giraffe-skin coat, and drank wine that tasted like a frosty day.'.

'Frosty morning,' Hiller corrected him.

And he remembered the Good Time then. He remembered the coat and the wine. For a moment he couldn't speak.

'It began with the postman coming up the path,' the boy said, 'with this magic card.'

'The mighty magic Excess Card.' Hiller nodded. He remembered that too. 'There were all those pretty pictures in the envelope, weren't there? Farmers getting shiny tractors. Insurance men getting speedboats, and televisions, and go-go girls of their choice.'

'That's it. And who was it who sent it to us?'

'A man who was a Mason and an Elk and a Mongoose,' Hiller said, 'and who managed the Midland Bank in his spare time. He told us we were Valued And Selected Customers, and would we please go out and spend £800?'

'And did we?' the boy asked. 'Did we spend all that?'

'Yes. It was nice being Valued And Selected Customers,' Hiller said. He remembered all of it now. The crazy weekend when he'd tried to patch up the marriage.

'And the wine that tasted like a frosty morning,' the boy said. 'You were the one who let me taste that, weren't you?'

'No,' Hiller lied, 'it was the Princess.'

'It wasn't,' the boy said. 'She said it would be wasted on a child. And she wouldn't take me to that cinema either. It was you who took me there.'

'Well, there were some things she didn't understand,' Hiller said.

'But it was always you. You made me the fort and the pirate's cave, you told me the stories in bed, you let me listen to Mahler's Fifth Symphony when I couldn't sleep, you . . .'

Suddenly Hiller stared at the back of the small brown head. It was pumping up and down, 'Christ.' He got up and pulled him close. 'What's the matter?'

And it was only then he saw the white lines of strain around the mouth. The eyes. The burden there.

'The Princess,' the boy whispered, 'she didn't really . . . want me, did she?'

'Who said. . . ?'

But Hiller knew. The only person he'd told that to. Ever.

He turned. He heard the silence that stretched over the partition wall, heard the woman sitting very still on the far side, listening. The woman with two suitcases and a child . . .

£40,000.

But he'd never understood about people and money. He couldn't be sure.

And then he was.

The boy took his wrist, looked at his watch. 'There's not much time, is there?'

'No.'

'Turn out your pockets.'

'What?'

'Turn out your pockets.'

Hiller did so. There was a handkerchief, a Sheaffer pen, a pipe, a leather tobacco pouch, matches, and an old Austrian lighter.

'Can I keep something?' the boy asked. 'Can I keep it for ever?'

Hiller nodded. He couldn't speak.

And the boy chose the oldest, most useless object. The

166

tarnished Austrian lighter that didn't work, that Hiller had carried around with him for years in case he found a new spring. An EBGO lighter.

Every Bugger's Got One.

A cold black rage went through Hiller. He stood up, and he saw the room again. The plaster that had fallen, the table with the broken lamp. There was no-one in this whole decaying house he could trust.

'Wait there,' he said to the boy. 'Don't you move a bloody inch.'

He went through the next room. Anna looked up from the bed. Her face told him nothing. 'It's not just yet, is it?' she asked.

'No. There's time,' Hiller said.

He went back down to the darkness of the hall. He went to the back door, but the Donkey was there, his hand in his pocket round his gun. He went to the front door, but it was boarded up. As were all the windows facing the sea.

There's time.

Under the stairs was the door of the cellar. He went through, closed it behind him, and switched on the light.

He saw the pile of coke across the brick floor. He saw the coal-chute above it, and he went over. There was a wooden trap door, weathered and rotten, he got it open. The sudden daylight made him blink. He was on the exposed side of the house, looking across the waste land to the sheds.

So he could get the boy out this way. But – and he heard the footsteps on the floor above – there were the men. The Guv'nor, Peterman, Donkey and Stoppo. All with guns. He began searching for something, he didn't know what, some weapon. *There's time.*

He came to the cylinders of Calor Gas by the cellar steps. He tapped them. One was empty. One was half-full, connected to the pipe that went to the kitchen. And the last one was full. They were large standing cylinders, nearly five feet high. Like bombs.

Not that. His hands shook. He turned away and searched on through the junk, the hat-boxes, the gas-masks from the war.

Gas. He looked back at the three cylinders. Not that.

But there wasn't any more time.

He didn't believe it as he took the large Stilson spanner to the valve of the empty cylinder. He heard the hiss, smelt the gas, as he got the core-plug out. And he counted the number of threads on the core. Seventeen.

He turned to the full cylinder. He levered it up onto the topmost of the steps, then slid it horizontally until it was wedged against a wooden upright. He made it firm with an old hydraulic jack he found on the floor. The head of the cylinder – the core-plug – was now directly under the cellar door.

For a moment he couldn't get his hands to work. For a moment he knew it was insane. But then he picked up the Stilson spanner. And slowly he unscrewed the core-plug. Of the full cylinder. Sixteen turns. Sixteen-and-a-quarter.

He put the spanner down and looked around. He looked from the bulb hanging in the middle of the cellar to the fuse-box on the wall. He went to the box and opened it up. At the third try he found the right fuse. The light went out.

There was just enough daylight from the open trap door for him to see. He had a length of wire – thick fence wire – in his hand. He laid it across the terminals, and put the fuse back. Then he went to the bulb in the centre of the room. He wrenched it off, stripped the rotten insulation from the flex, and left the bare wires hanging together, just touching.

29

They were standing outside the back door in the shadow of the house. A section of the gutter was broken, and the wall was slimy with rain.

It was just before two. The men were watching Hiller now, hands in their pockets, expecting trouble.

A gust of wind came down the side of the house. It peeled back the flap of Hiller's hair. His head was square suddenly, set forward. There was the same bulldog quality that came to him when he had a mathematical problem. And that's all it was now – five against one.

Or four against two. He went to where Salto stood, and spoke very quietly: 'You remember what you said back in the flat? If there was trouble, you'd help with the boy?'

Salto's face showed nothing. There was just the flicker of fear in his eyes.

'You go first then,' Hiller said, 'with Anna and Mo. Go to where the van is, and keep going, whatever happens here.'

He left Salto then and went back to where the boy was. The Guv'nor and the Donkey moved in towards him, their right hands never leaving their pockets.

'Two o'clock,' the Guv'nor said. 'Let's go.'

Salto picked up his briefcase. He went away round the corner with Anna and Mo. Hiller heard them cross the small garden, go out through the gate. He gave them time to reach the waste land on the way to the sheds. Then he grabbed up the boy.

And they'd expected him to go the other way, after Salto. He had three yards start as he went back into the house, six as he slammed the kitchen door. He ran down the hall, ducked left, and got the cellar door open. Then he picked up the boy, one-handed, by the scruff of the neck.

The sweat poured off him as he stepped over the Calor Gas cylinder on the step. He was swaying with the weight of the boy, feeling with his foot. Then he put the boy down and shut the door, slid home the bolts.

It was dark. He heard the men behind him slamming into the door. And he carried the boy on, across the cellar to the pile of coke. He pushed him up to the top of it, his head poking out into the grey day. 'Now you run, towards those sheds. *Run*.'

The boy started off. Hiller went back across the cellar, to the gas cylinder on the step. He picked up the large Stil-son spanner and fitted it to the core-plug, tightened it. The heavy shaft of the spanner came up to the bottom of the door.

And the door shook suddenly. The Guv'nor had some kind of a ram on the far side. 'Fuggoff,' he shouted to the others. 'Give me fugging room.'

Hiller's hand went out to the light switch. But he couldn't do it. There was bone and gristle on the far side. Still all in one piece.

Then the bone and gristle shouted: 'You're dead. Both of you. You hear that? Dead.'

Hiller pressed the switch.

And he ran, past the sparking wires in the centre of the cellar. He scrabbled up the pile of coke and went out.

The ram thudded into the door. A bolt snapped off. The ram came again.

The door burst open, hitting the spanner. There was a huge roar as liquid became gas, rushing at the electric spark.

Hiller was on top of the boy, shielding him.

The blast took them ten feet across the ground, tearing their hands. The noise went on and on. Then there were bricks, chunks of masonry, smacking down all round them. Hiller heard something hit his arm, the dull sound of it, but he didn't feel pain.

He looked back.

The whole side of the house had fallen away. Rooms, fireplaces, sagged open to the sky. A bed hung down in the dustcloud.

He looked on, at the other houses in the terrace. He saw the women coming out into front gardens, the little knots of them.

'Get going.' He pushed the boy towards the sheds.

The van was reversing towards them, Salto at the wheel. He got out. 'Jesus Christ. What in Christ's name have you done?'

And Hiller didn't know.

Then he saw the figure coming out of the dust, shambling, wounded.

The Donkey.

And Hiller began to hope. Because the Donkey would have been second in line behind the Guv'nor. *Give me fugging room.* And maybe he'd been back in the hall. Maybe the main structure had held.

The Donkey stood in the middle of the road. He got the gun out of his pocket and he raised it with both hands. Behind him were the women in their gardens. The white mist over the sea. A train passing. And people standing at the windows, unsurprised. They wouldn't believe until the nine o'clock news.

A puff of dust kicked up to Hiller's right.

'Come on,' Salto shouted.

'What d'you mean?'

'What do I *mean*?' Salto hauled him into the van.

30

They drove fast, and it was insane. Because the land was flat, and there was mist rolling in from the sea, thick patches that covered the road. They overtook a car, and then a lorry beyond. Headlights came at them suddenly, a hooter rising to a shriek. But Salto got through, his hands shaking on the wheel. And behind him Anna crouched down with Mo, saying nothing.

Until they saw the yellow lights of the shops ahead.

'Pull up,' she shouted.

'For Christ's sake,' Salto said. 'the Law's been rung by now.'

'Pull *up*.'

He did so, and she got out. She was reaching back for Mo, when Hiller stopped her. He got out too, and closed the van door.

'What d'you think you're doing?'

'*Doing*?' She tried to get the door open. 'I'm getting off. With Mo.'

'You mean, what happened back there?' He was shaking. 'All right, there was one person killed, others hurt. But it was them or me.'

'Open that door.' She tore at his hand.

'For God's sake, there's a plane leaving in half an hour. You've got to come with us. Don't you see that?'

'No.'

Then he stared at her. 'It's not what happened back there, is it?'

'What?' For a moment she was still.

'It's *why* it happened. You're scared of me now. You

172

reckon I know. About you and the money.'

And he saw he was right.

'I do know.' He sighed. 'But it doesn't make any difference. You can still have half, like I promised. Just get back in the van.'

But he wasn't prepared for her savagery.

'You pig-noble bloody . . .' Her nails flew at his face. '. . . You think I can take it from you now?'

He caught her wrists. 'I wasn't doing it for you,' he said. 'It's Mo. For Mo's good.'

'For Mo's *good*?'

And suddenly he drew back, frightened.

She came after him, her head tilted strangely on one side. 'I tried to tell you about Mo, didn't I?' she said. 'That night back in the flat. But you didn't want to believe me.'

Then he remembered. The strange things she'd . . .

'I told you it was possible to know the time Mo came from. The rotten stinking time, and I'm talking about bed . . . I told you I could have prevented Mo, but I didn't . . . And I suppose you thought it was like some beautiful flower coming out of the stinking manure.'

She stood there in the mist, her hair falling dark around her face.

'I once knew a man who ran a construction company,' she said. 'There was a day when he took his kid onto the site. The kid walked into a winch handle. And this man, he took the kid with him everywhere after it had come out of hospital. Restaurants, shops, everywhere. He had to show him, with his head caved in.'

Hiller made no move to stop her as she opened the van door. She got the little girl out. They walked away towards the yellow lights. Until they were swallowed up by the mist.

Then there were just the three of them in the van. They were driving in open country, the mist coming in swirls, the hedges flatter as they neared the sea. The road ended suddenly in a carpark with wide black puddles. There were signs, KARTING, KRAZY GOLF.

Salto got out with his briefcase. Hiller and the boy hurried behind. They passed two low concrete buildings, Reception and Yer-Tiz. Then Salto was calling back to them.

'Come on, Heart. It's only round the point here. Just keep thinking of that plane.'

'But what about the mist? No plane'll get off in this.'

Salto didn't answer.

They came to the sea wall, a long dyke of grey stones, as round as eggs. Salto scrambled up on it. 'There's wind up here,' he said. 'And it's clearer round the point. You can see a long way.'

Then Hiller stopped. 'What's that?'

'What's what?'

'Sounded like a car.'

They both listened.

'No,' Salto said. 'Maybe a ship out at sea.'

They went on, Hiller and the boy below the dyke in the spikey salt-grass. Salto above them, the stones chinkling away from his heels. Twice more Hiller stopped, thinking he could hear voices.

They came to a hollow. There were bathing huts, row after row of them, their paint flaking, their roofs wired down to cement weights. They were set in a triangle at the tip of the point.

'Where are we going?' the boy asked.

'Switzerland,' Hiller said.

'Do we know people there?'

'No.'

'We're the only people that we know,' the boy said.

He walked on, one foot on each of two gull-tracks in the sand, his legs getting further and further apart.

There was a crack. Salto came spilling down the side of the dyke with the stones.

He lay there, sand on his suede coat, holding himself quite still. Hiller saw the stain where the coat was open, high up on the shirt.

174

The boy stared.

Hiller bent quickly and buttoned up the coat. He'd forgotten about the headline: SURREY PC DIES. The police were armed. Behind him now there were footsteps on the shingle.

Salto seemed to gather himself. He got up on one elbow and reached out for Hiller. He looked around with an animal's cunning. And he saw the long pool that stretched from the dyke to the beach huts.

They went through it, leaving no tracks on the sand. All of Salto's weight was on Hiller, but his strength was still there, pushing them both on past hut after hut, row after row. Then he was weaker. They went in through a door.

It was quiet suddenly. Salto lay straight out across the bare wooden floor. There was the smell of American cloth, of paraffin.

And it was now that Hiller expected him to cry out, to show something. For Christ's sake, at the age of twenty-seven, a bullet inside him, dying?

But the control was still there. Salto just stared up at him, every whisker separate on his waxy skin.

'Get . . . the boy out.'

'What?'

'Get him . . . *out*.' A tiny flicker of anger.

And then Hiller knew, what the control was. It was the boy in Salto that had never been, the summer evenings in some park somewhere he'd never had.

Hiller did as he was told. He took the boy to the door.

Then he heard the tapping behind him. The faint tapping.

He turned. Salto's fingers were pointing at the airline briefcase. Hiller went back and picked it up.

'Take . . . what . . . . you . . . want.'

'What?' Hiller bent over him.

But Salto couldn't speak. Compartments inside him were breaking up.

Hiller led the boy outside. He closed the door.

Then he swung round. He heard the other doors

banging open and shut away down the line. Far away. They were having to move slowly, search through each hut in turn.

Hiller hitched the briefcase to his belt. He slung the boy over his shoulder and he ran, in the other direction. He skirted a dune, then he kept to the low ground behind the dyke, where the mist was.

Suddenly there was an embankment ahead of them, the railway that followed the coast. They went over the rails and saw the field beyond, the square shape of a barn.

A man was standing in the doorway, slapping himself with gloved hands. There was a plane behind him in the shadows.

'Who in hell are you?' The voice was Canadian.

Hiller put the boy down. He couldn't speak.

'The guy said there were six of you.'

'Only two,' Hiller panted. 'Two of us left now.'

The Canadian stared at him strangely. Then he pointed out at the field. 'You want me to fly you out in this?'

'I suppose . . . .'

'You suppose what, for Chrissakes? We get off and keep to the hills, keep off the radar screens, like always? So tell me how in hell we *do* get off? It's down to about a hundred yards out there. You can't see the goddam trees, can you?'

Hiller didn't answer.

Then they both heard it. The whistle from the far side of the embankment. The police whistle.

'Chrissakes, you want me to fly in this?'

There was another whistle. Nearer.

'Move ass.' The Canadian got the plane door open.

Hiller was back in the second row of seats, strapped in with the boy. In front of them the Canadian was swearing, on and on. Then they couldn't hear him any more. The engines bellowed on either side. They rumbled over the field.

They hit mist, thick and white. It went on and on.

'*Chrissakes.*' They heard just the one word. The rumbling stopped. They lifted off. Blind.

Suddenly the tree, straight ahead.

The Canadian pulled the stick over. Hiller knew they would stall. But the engines screamed, sucking them up through the white. Until . . .

They were up in a huge pale sunset. As wide as the world.

31

On the far side of the lake the mountains were snow-covered, bright in the winter sun. Hiller walked in shadow where the trams ground past the solid Swiss business houses. He came to the bank.

His heels clicked on the polished marble floor as he went to the window marked Withdrawals, Change, Gold.

'I have an account with you,' he said.

'Yes, sir?'

'A numbered account,' he lowered his voice.

The clerk passed him a piece of paper.

And on it Hiller wrote 792753.

The clerk turned to a small keyboard by his side. He stamped out 7–9–2–7–5–3.

Hiller waited. In Salto's briefcase there'd been six passports. And in each of them a slip of paper with an Account Number, and an amount.

A light winked above the clerk's head.

'Would you go up to the second floor, please, sir? Someone will meet you.'

Hiller went where he'd pointed. He passed a man standing further along the counter. A man who could have been just close enough to hear.

The second floor foyer was thickly carpeted, there were original paintings on the walls. 'Good morning, sir.' The girl at the desk smiled at him. 'Could I have your Account Number, please?'

'792753.'

'Thank you. Would you kindly wait in Room 3?'

Room 3 had a large boardroom table, Hepplewhite chairs, and again the originals on the walls, smelling of oil-paint. The same girl came in. 'Did you want to see your statement, sir?'

'No,' Hiller said, 'I want to make a withdrawal.'

She went out. In a few minutes a man came in. 'Could I have your name, sir, please?'

'Kaminsky,' Hiller said.

The man had a small file card in his hand, he glanced at it. 'And your passport number?'

'Oh.' Hiller took the green American passport from his pocket. '886246.'

'And once again, please, your Account Number?'

'792753.'

'Thank you, sir. How much was it you wished to withdraw?'

'£40,000.'

It was the whole amount, but the man didn't blink. 'Would you like that in Swiss Francs?'

'Yes, please,' Hiller said.

And in fifteen minutes he had it, in a small black case with steel locks.

He put the case in a left-luggage locker at the station. Then he went to another bank.

He walked past its doorway once, he walked past it twice. In his pocket he had a second passport, with Salto's photograph on it. There was a second slip of paper too, giving an Account Number. 'Take what you want,' Salto had said. And Salto's share was two and a quarter million pounds.

Hiller went in. He walked over to the window marked

Withdrawals, Change, Gold. And as he did so, a man got up from a chair and came over to the next window. A man who was standing close enough to hear.

Sod's Law.

Two hours later Hiller arrived back at the Canadian's flat. It was light-panelled, with a wide window overlooking the lake. The Canadian was showing the boy pictures of aeroplanes. He saw the new suitcase Hiller was carrying, he saw the two black attaché cases with steel locks.

And he recognised those.

He came over. 'Five-hundred pounds for a morning's baby-sitting,' he said quietly. 'That's a lot of money. Maybe we should talk.'

Hiller put the suitcase down. He let his jacket hang free, let the weight hang free in his right pocket.

'You heard there was shooting, didn't you?' he said.

The man shook his head. He backed away.

Hiller's hand went into his pocket. He felt the large adjustable spanner he'd bought in the department store. It had been a good thought.

He took the boy through to the bedroom and opened the suitcase. There were parcels inside. A dark sober suit, a blue shirt, and a knitted tie. There were handmade shoes, a Sinatra hat, and a lightweight overcoat with small checks. It was Hiller's idea of how an American would dress. He took the overcoat and rubbed it against the dirty carpet by the door.

'What you doing that for?' the boy asked.

'Come here a moment,' Hiller said. 'I've got some clothes for you as well.' He was nervous suddenly.

The boy unwrapped the first parcel. 'No,' he said.

'Look, I want you to wear it. It's only for tonight. One night.'

'No.'

Hiller caught hold of him. 'I've never hit you before, have I? Ever.'

179

'*No*,' the boy said. 'Bloody *girl's* clothes?'
And Hiller let him go.
Sod's Law. You Can't Win.

32

Police sirens followed them as they drove out of the city. Hiller kept down in the back of the car with the boy. He got the Canadian to go on past the airport, and then double back at the next turning. The sirens had gone by the time they drew up near the Departures Building. But Hiller still kept down.

Then it was time. There were ten minutes left before the flight was called. Hiller got out of the car with the suitcase and took the boy's hand. Glass doors opened up in front of him, and he didn't look back.

He felt very tired suddenly as he walked under the needle-point lights and the muzak. They seemed very far away. He went to the Pan-Am desk, and didn't even attempt an American accent as he explained . . . There were five round-trip tickets under the name of Kaminsky. Could he get a refund on three of them as half the family had 'flu?

'Oh, God.' The girl looked round at the clock. 'Look, keep the tickets with you for now. Something will have to be fixed up in flight.'

Hiller put the suitcase on the scales. A Pan-Am label was slapped on it, and he watched £2,290,000 in Swiss Francs being carried away.

Then, as he picked up his tickets, he saw the girl nod at someone behind him. He turned. A man was walking off. It could have been a boyfriend, anyone.

Hiller took the boy quickly away.

'You walk down any street in Europe with that kid,'

Salto had said, 'and you get done.'

Hiller knew he'd got it all wrong now. Coming straight to Switzerland, walking into two Swiss banks. He felt angry as he joined the crowd by the tourist shops, as he looked at watches and bars of chocolate.

The Pan-Am flight was called. Hiller turned and stared at the queue. He didn't want to go over there. Not yet. He led the boy on to the toy counter.

They stopped by a small model yacht. The boy ran his fingers over it. 'That cabin cruiser, radio-controlled,' he said. 'Will you get me another one?'

Yes, Hiller said, he would.

He looked at the Pan-Am queue again. It was thinning out. He started towards it with the boy.

Then he stopped.

Because beyond the Customs Officials and the man at the Passport Control, there was another man, in a light fawn raincoat. The only man who wasn't in uniform.

And it could have been a check for hi-jackers. Except that he wasn't looking at anyone in the queue. He was just waiting.

Sod's Law.

The flight was called again, for the last time. Hiller had to go on. He stood at the end of the queue with the boy, and he got out his American passport. Stephen Kaminsky had three children, Sue, Louella, and Stephen Jr . . . Salto had done his best.

But it wasn't going to be enough. He knew it as he reached the uniformed man at the Control. And as the man in the fawn raincoat came up on the far side of the counter, looking at Hiller and looking away.

'Your passport, please.' The uniformed man took it. He checked the photo with Hiller's face. Then he flipped through two or three pages.

'The other children aren't travelling with you, Mr Kaminsky?'

No, Hiller said, they weren't.

The man still held onto the passport. And then the man

in the fawn coat leaned over his shoulder. He whispered something.

Hiller stood quite still. The whispering stopped. The uniformed man gave back the passport.

Hiller took it, and walked on. As he did so, he saw the man in the raincoat go over to a phone on the wall. He was getting help. They were going to take Hiller either in the bus or on the plane.

Sod's Law.

Out in the darkness, the roar of jets, the boy was excited. He pressed his face against the bus window and stared at the lights of the planes. 'You said we were going up in a airliner. You said that, didn't you?'

Yes, Hiller said, he had.

They drove out towards the gangway. They got out and walked up the steps.

And inside, in the hiss of air-conditioning, the soft music, the boy walked proudly between the seats. The air hostess found him a window, she showed him how to fasten his seat-belt. Hiller did the same.

And he waited.

There was quiet around him, everyone was in their seats. And still he waited.

Then he looked back.

The plane door was still open. And the man in the fawn coat was there, leaning in.

Hiller shrank back into his seat. He saw the air hostess coming towards him, saw her smile.

'Would your little boy like to come up to the cockpit while we're waiting? To see the controls?'

They were getting the boy away from him, before they made their move.

No, Hiller said, he wanted the boy to stay.

'Can't I?' The boy leaned forward. 'Can't I go?'

The air hostess unfastened his seat-belt. She took him away.

Hiller looked back again at the man in the fawn coat. He was staring straight at him.

You Just Can't Win.

Then things happened quickly.

The man in the fawn coat ducked back. Another man came in past him and up the aisle. He was carrying a metal case, white with a red cross on it. He took it up to the steward's alcove ahead of Hiller and put it in the fridge. Then he went out.

The man in the fawn coat disappeared. The door closed.

'Sorry about the delay. We were waiting for organ transplants.' The air hostess was back with the boy. She sat him in his seat and re-fastened his belt.

The whine of the engines rose. They went out to the turning-circle.

The boy was frightened, forced back into his seat by the take-off. Then they were climbing, the lights far below through the window.

'Where are we going?' the boy asked.

'Mexico,' Hiller said.

'Mexico? D'you think we'll see Pissoff the Peon?'

'Bound to.' Hiller found he was crying. 'Bloody bound to.'

Also available
from Thames Mandarin

JOHN BURKE

The Bill

Wapping, in the East End of London, is a tough
manor. A typical day has dippers in the High
Street, break-ins to cars and homes, lost dogs and
runaway kids. The patch has its fair share of
more serious crime too – drugs, armed robbery,
porn. For PC Carver, fresh from Hendon,
Sergeant Cryer, Detective Inspector Galloway
and the rest of the Bill based at Sun Hill Police
Station, there is no respite. And the not-always-
friendly rivalry between uniformed and plain-
clothes branches does little to ease tension . . .

LYNDA LA PLANTE

Widows 2

Dolly Rawlins, Shirley Miller, Linda Pirelli and Bella O'Reilly set out to do the impossible, hold up an armed security wagon.

Using Dolly Rawlins' husband's plans, they succeed and make their escape to Rio, leaving the bulk of their cash hidden in London. The women are free, rich, and ready to start a new life. When the scream has died down, they will return to share out their cash. Only the shadow of the man they had presumed dead hangs over them.

Harry Rawlins is alive, and he wants the women's money – and he will go to any lengths to retrieve what he feels is rightly his, even more so when he discovers his 'widow' has laid claim to all his business and banking assets.

Rawlins is desperate to find his wife and through her the haul from the robbery. The hunt is on and the widows' freedom short-lived . . .

A Selected List of Fiction Available from Mandarin Books

While every effort is made to keep prices low, it is sometimes necessary to increase prices at short notice. Mandarin Paperbacks reserves the right to show new retail prices on covers which may differ from those previously advertised in the text or elsewhere.

The prices shown below were correct at the time of going to press.

☐	7493 0003 5	**Mirage**	James Follett	£3.99
☐	7493 0005 1	**China Saga**	C. Y. Lee	£3.50
☐	7493 0009 4	**Larksghyll**	Constance Heaven	£2.99
☐	7493 0012 4	**The Falcon of Siam**	Axel Aylwyn	£3.99
☐	7493 0018 3	**Daughter of the Swan**	Joan Juliet Buck	£3.50
☐	7493 0020 5	**Pratt of the Argus**	David Nobbs	£3.50
☐	7493 0025 6	**Here Today**	Zoë Fairbairns	£3.50

TV and Film Titles

☐	7493 0002 7	**The Bill III**	John Burke	£2.99
☐	7493 0055 8	**Neighbours I**	Marshall/Kolle	£2.99
☐	423 02020 X	**Bellman and True**	Desmond Lowden	£2.50
☐	416 13972 8	**Why the Whales Came**	Michael Morpurgo	£2.50
☐	7493 0017 5	**Adventures of Baron Munchausen**	McKeown/Gilliam	£2.99

All these books are available at your bookshop or newsagent, or can be ordered direct from the publisher. Just tick the titles you want and fill in the form below.

Mandarin Paperbacks, Cash Sales Department, PO Box 11, Falmouth, Cornwall TR10 9EN.

Please send cheque or postal order, no currency, fo₁ purchase price quoted and allow the following for postage and packing:

UK	55p for the first book, 22p for the second book and 14p for each additional book ordered to a maximum charge of £1.75.
BFPO and Eire	55p for the first book, 22p for the second book and 14p for each of the next seven books, thereafter 8p per book.
Overseas Customers	£1.00 for the first book plus 25p per copy for each additional book.

NAME (Block Letters) ....

ADDRESS ....

....